HE SAID SHE SAID

shawn
&
rachel

Shannon Layne

EPIC
Press

Shawn & Rachel
He Said She Said: Book #4

Written by Shannon Layne

Copyright © 2016 by Abdo Consulting Group, Inc.

Published by EPIC Press™
PO Box 398166
Minneapolis, MN 55439

Cover design and illustration by Candice Keimig
Edited by Marianna Baer

LIBRARY OF CONGRESS CATALOGING-IN-PUBLICATION DATA

Layne, Shannon.
Shawn & Rachel / Shannon Layne.
p. cm. — (He said, she said)
Summary: Shawn and Rachel meet on the lakeshore and fall headfirst into something
neither is prepared for. Meanwhile, a secret lies beneath the surface, which will make
these two lovers find common ground in the eye of the storm.
ISBN 978-1-68076-039-2 (hardcover)
1. Camps—Fiction. 2. Summer romance—Fiction. 3. Interpersonal relations—
Fiction. 4. High school students—Fiction. 5. Young adult fiction. I. Title.
[Fic]—dc23
2015932727

EPICPRESS.COM

For my dad, who never fails to make me laugh.
I love you to the end of the world.

rachel

Since I was a little girl, I've watched men walk in and out of my mother's life. There was the guy from the barber shop for a while, then the one who worked at the bakery on 5th, and the blonde one who took off a wedding ring and dropped it on our side table every time he came over. They became faceless to me after a while, just an endless parade of men who I sometimes awkwardly bumped into when I was trying to get a glass of orange juice before school. I watched my mother fall hopelessly for every single one, and I watched every single one leave. As I listened to my mother sob in the bedroom next to mine for what felt like the thousandth time, I vowed that I wouldn't be like her. I wouldn't be the one left crying and alone. I would be whoever I wanted, but never that.

shawn

Luke used to ask for waffles with peanut butter for every single meal. He could never turn down a dare, and he was always tugging on my hand toward a new adventure. That's how I always remember him. Not with plastic crisscrossing every part of his skin. Not when he was gasping for every breath on a respirator.

"Hey, buddy," I remember saying as I sat beside the bed. He was sitting up, fiddling with the blanket. His shoulders were hunched forward, his back so thin now that I could count the knobs of his spine.

"I just wanna go skateboarding," he said quietly. "I want to go outside."

We both turned to look at the multitude of plastic lines and needles—one IV in his hand, another attached to his chest, the oxygen tube for his nose. His breath was a rattling wheeze, but at least he wasn't hooked up to the respirator at that point.

"I know," I said, leaning my elbows on my knees. "I wish I could take you."

"Why can't you?"

Our parents were off consulting with a doctor somewhere; there were no nurses in sight. Luke was barely six and sat there staring at me like an adult. His eyes were huge in his face, dark brown like mine. I could see him fading in front of me, and we had already heard what the doctors had to say. His organs were beginning to shut down. The cancer had spread to his kidneys.

"Good question," I said.

I picked him up off the bed effortlessly, taking a few seconds to unhook all of his IV's. The alarms were already starting to beep from all the detached machines, but we both ignored them. The oxygen I hooked up to a portable tank, hurrying to get it attached before the nurses arrived and stopped us. Luke was grinning so hard it looked like his face might split in half.

"I can walk," he said, pushing my arms away, and I set him down.

I grabbed the hospital blanket and we strolled out of there as casual as can be, and not a single person stopped us.

Luke rolled down every single window in the car. He pulled the oxygen tubes from his nose and breathed the air in with huge breaths, his chest rising and falling. It was so much better than the stale air of the hospital.

I think that's what I remember most. Luke's hands out the window, the sun on his face. He was smiling so hard. In that moment, before our parents and the doctor came after us and forced us back to the hospital, he wasn't sick. He was Luke again.

CHAPTER 1
rachel

I didn't expect the air to be so different here. It smells different, feels different on my skin. I swear it feels different in my lungs, like with each breath I'm clearing out more and more of the Manhattan smog. I asked the cab driver to roll down the windows as soon as I got into the car, and he looked at me like I was insane. But Saranac Lake is the most beautiful place I've ever seen. We passed the town a little while back, with the old Victorian houses and brick storefronts, and now we're headed to the edge of the lake where the camp is held. As we are driving, I catch flashes of dark blue water through the trees. Everything seems so green despite the fact that it's summer, like I'm in the middle of a mystical place completely separate from reality.

We're still heading down a winding dirt road, and the trees are getting thicker except for openings in the forest where I can see clearings and patches of flowers. I wonder if there are bears here. Funny, I wasn't asked anything about my ability to defend myself from wild animals when I applied to be a counselor. I never thought that I would actually be chosen—there are a limited number of spots for counselors in each section, and Poetry is one of the most difficult to get into.

I wonder if Mom remembered to get up and go to work or if she's still on the couch. I feel guilty for looking forward to a few months away from her. I feel guilty just writing it down. But as soon as I got into the car I thought I could be free for a little while. I can be anyone I want, not the skinny girl from the Bronx with no friends. It might not be forever, but it's as close as I can get.

A final jolt from the car yanks my pen from the page as the car comes to a stop.

"Thank you," I say, shoving money into the driver's hand as I climb out of the car. I pull my suitcase from where I had set it on the seat beside me and breathe in again. For the next three days it's just the counselors, going through orientation before the campers arrive. The air is pleasantly warm and I know the sun will probably burn my freckled shoulders before I know it, but I don't care.

I slam the door and the driver pulls away instantly, briefly enveloping me in a cloud of dust. I cough and step toward the noise of voices and footsteps, dragging my enormous suitcase. It's the only suitcase I have, and it's ancient. With my backpack already on my shoulders, it's a lot to drag. I sigh and hoist it against my body and head toward the chaos. As I near the mass of adults and people who look to be about my age, my lungs seem to be having a difficult time expanding properly.

I pause at the outer perimeter of the crowd of people, dropping my suitcase onto one of the piles of bags strewn throughout the campground. A huge wooden sign hangs over the whole area with the words "Camp Maple Leaf" in carved wooden letters. Camp is two weeks long, and it's one of the most selective summer camps for the arts on the east coast. Both potential campers and counselors apply under a specific emphasis: Drama, Dance, Visual Arts, Music, and Creative Writing. In the Creative Writing category you can choose either Poetry or Fiction. Every camper participates in activities for every category, but counselors only supervise the specific activity they applied under and then the general ones for their cabin, like hiking and swimming.

I see the adult counselors with their clipboards and green shirts, and then a scattering of dark blue shirts like the one I have on, which means other youth counselors. There is an adult counselor assigned to each cabin to work with the youth counselors and make sure everything is going smoothly. They handle the whole management aspect of camp—at least, that's what my introductory email said. I pull the bill of my cap down further over my eyes and start forward again.

A tall, thin woman with salt-and-pepper hair cut into a bob is holding a clipboard and addressing a group of people in blue shirts. I head in her direction.

"A new face! I'm sorry, dear, you must have been absent when we made the first introductions."

"Yeah," I say, as everyone's face turns in my direction. "My cab was late. I'm sorry."

"Quite all right, quite all right," she murmurs, flipping through her clipboard. "And you must be Rachel. I'm Ms. Nancy."

It is still a shock to hear someone call me by that name, but my real name is Mercedes and I've never stopped loathing it. I honestly think my mom might have still been high on pain medication when she named me. Rachel, on the other hand, was my grandmother's name, and it sounded so sophisticated and regal when I said it out loud that I put it down on my application instead of my awful real name.

A redhead to my right gives me a small grin, and I smile back, adjusting the straps of the backpack on my shoulders. Ms. Nancy flips another page over on her clipboard. She's sorting us into our cabins—we weren't told ahead of time. I think it's a process to prevent anyone from fighting an assignment before camp has even begun. I've requested a cabin with our youngest age group, the six- to eight-year-olds. They have the most energy and are often among the hardest to control, but they're so simple. I babysit a little girl who lives in the apartment next to me and love it. Mostly I just try to get her to do her homework and entertain her until her mom gets off work. Little kids don't have real problems yet. It's so much easier to comfort a little girl who is upset because she dropped her Popsicle in the dirt.

"Rachel? Yes, dear, there you are," says Ms. Nancy as I throw my hand up in the air and manage to slap the person in front of me in the back of the head. I've gone approximately five minutes without embarrassing myself.

"Sorry," I whisper.

"You've got the Otter Tail cabin, Rachel, ages six to eight. And your counselor buddy is going to be . . . " She flips another page. "Alexis. Alexis, dear? Why don't you raise your hand so Rachel knows which one you are."

She peers down her glasses into the crowd of us and a pale arm flies into the air, fingers waving gracefully. Following the arm to its owner, I see the cloud of red hair and realize it's the same girl who smiled at me when I walked up to the group. Ms. Nancy is handing us all packets of paper stapled together and shooing us toward a table set up to the right of the camp entrance. The table is covered with plain clipboards and extra tank tops and T-shirts in the blue that I know I'll be sick of by the time camp ends. Sandwiched in a cluster of counselors, I manage to snag a clipboard and a few more tank tops.

"Head to the mess hall after you've grabbed your packets and clipboards," Ms. Nancy is calling above the babble of voices. "Orientation will continue there! Grab your partner!"

Everybody begins to split up into groups of two or three, depending on the size of their cabins. I crane my neck looking for my partner until there's a tap on my shoulder.

"Rachel?" I spin around. She has silky red hair that's bright as embers but somehow still gorgeous. Her eyes are dark green and crinkle as she smiles, as does her nose, which has a sprinkle of freckles. I feel like an ogre next to her.

"Hi," I say, tongue-tied. I don't make new friends very often. "You're Alexis?"

"Ugh, Lexi, please. My mom calls me Alexis. Hi, nice to meet you."

As she shakes my hand vigorously I notice her voice has a lilt, and some of her vowels are drawn out. When she speaks it's like music.

"Do you have an accent?"

"Oh, yes," she sighs, flipping her hair over her shoulder. "Texas, born and bred. But my mama grew up here in New York. She went to camp here when she was little."

"Oh. I see."

I try to picture my mother camping in the woods and can't come close. As far as I know, she's never left the city, and certainly never stayed anywhere she couldn't go grab another bottle of vodka at any time of night.

"Were you hoping for the little ones, too?" Lexi asks.

"Yes," I answer.

"Me too. I have a sister who's barely a year younger than me and I want to murder her on a daily basis. The babies are easier."

Lexi marches us toward the mess hall, looping her arm through mine.

"So what's your emphasis?" she asks.

"Creative Writing," I answer. "Poetry, not Fiction."

"Oh, wow," says Lexi. "I'm a dancer, myself. This is my first year here."

"Me too," I say.

"This place is a lot bigger than I expected," says Lexi approvingly.

"I know," I say, but my voice isn't quite so brave. I'm overwhelmed by the sheer amount of space, the neat rows of cabins.

"We'll figure it out in no time," says Lexi brightly. "Come on. We should hurry up."

As she tugs me along, I'm glad Lexi seems more confident than me. I already feel lost amid the sea of counselors, and the campers aren't even here yet. I wring my hands and start to gnaw on a thumbnail until I catch myself. I breathe in deeply, catching a breath of cool wind blowing off the lake. I force my muscles to relax and toss my head back. Back at home, all I ever try to do is disappear. Maybe here I'll finally get the chance to start over.

CHAPTER 2
shawn

We're packed in the hot, stuffy mess hall like sardines in a can. The adults assigned to each of our cabins stand in a row at the front. Ms. Nancy is droning on about everything that she already emailed to us weeks ago, and I shift in my seat. I'm sitting next to my best friend, Jamie, who's been my counselor buddy for the past two years. We've known each other since we were little, went to kindergarten together and all that. He adjusts the glasses on his nose. Jamie looks like the biggest nerd. He's skinny and lanky and with those glasses he looks like he sits and reads in a library all day. But you would be surprised. He's got a mean pool game, and he's one of the best swimmers I've ever seen. He doesn't take shit from anyone. On top of that, he plays the piano like he was born to do it. I'm a sax player myself, but I've got a lot of respect for his talent.

My shirt is sticking to my chest. I glance around at the other counselors. Some are buddies of mine that have been counselors before, like me, but there are some new faces too. A redhead catches my eye and smiles, tossing her hair over her shoulder. I smile back, but briefly. She turns and whispers something to the brunette sitting beside her, and the brunette turns her head to look at me. She has dark hair that falls over a pale face. Her gaze locks with mine and she blushes immediately and parts her lips. She looks like a scared kitten debating whether to stay still or go hide under the kitchen table. I grin at her and she turns even more red and looks away. Her redhead friend immediately starts whispering in her ear again. What kind of girl is so shy that a look from a guy makes her blush?

Ms. Nancy starts outlining the structure of our days, going over each group's rotation, and how we'll move the campers through our stations. It's pretty simple: each cabin has a different rotation each day, and the stations depend on the counselors and the campers. Things like swimming, hiking, and arts and crafts are general activities that everyone takes part in. The kids meet up with their cabin counselors at various times during the day, but they also spend time with whatever counselor teaches their emphasis. It's mostly old news to me, so I lean back and wait for Ms. Nancy to wind down.

"During the next three days, we will talk more about schedules and make sure you all have your assignments for the two weeks of camp. But we will also spend time getting to know each other before the campers arrive. There will be a daytime swim on the dock later today, a volleyball tournament tomorrow, and finally a bonfire the night before the campers arrive."

I glance behind me again. The dark-haired girl is twisting her hair around her finger, and I can see where her wrist is covered with a smear of ink. She holds her hair off the back of her neck and a bead of sweat trickles from her neck and down the front of her shirt. She sighs and her chest strains against her tank top. She opens her eyes again and sees me staring. For a second she holds my gaze, and I smile at her, watching the blush creep up her neck. She settles back into her chair, throwing her shoulders against the back to let me know I've irritated her. I turn back as Ms. Nancy starts to split us up, picturing the bead of sweat on her neck.

Ms. Nancy divides us up into small groups to do name games and get to know each other a little more. Jamie is in a group with the brunette. Lucky bastard.

After hours of training and getting to know the other counselors, Ms. Nancy and the adult counselors release us to swim and hang out by the dock for an hour or so before it's time for dinner and bed. Jamie and I head to our empty cabin to change and then start down the trail to the water.

"Jeez, I thought we were never going to get out of there," says Jamie. He adjusts the glasses on his nose. "I think a blonde I saw at orientation is calling my name."

"Oh yeah? Does she want some Jamie magic?"

"You bet your ass she does. I can tell."

I punch his arm and he almost falls into the bushes on the side of the trail. I can't help but laugh for a second, even as he regains his footing and punches me back.

"I saw that redhead giving you the eye in the mess hall."

"Oh, yeah. I did too. She's pretty hot."

"Are you into her?"

"I don't know. We'll see."

"Her little brunette friend was interesting."

"Oh, yeah? I saw she was in one of your groups."

Jamie gives me a surprised look.

"Why do you care so much?"

"I don't. I was just curious."

"Well, I talked to her for a second while we were sitting there."

I'm not surprised. Jamie is the definition of a social butterfly.

"I asked her about the ink on her arm. She said she was writing during the cab ride here. She's a lefty, like me, so the ink gets all over the place. She's a Poetry emphasis."

Now my interest is caught. I might be here for music, but poetry is a big part of my family. My mom used to read us Walt Whitman before bed when we were little, which sounds strange, but I loved it. Since we lost Luke, I've written poems from time to time when I was really struggling. None of it is worth reading, I'm sure, but it still helped.

"She was pretty shy," continues Jamie. "She smiled a lot, though."

My throat goes tight at the mention of her smile.

CHAPTER 3
shawn

We make it to the lake where other counselors are already lying on towels on the warm wood of the dock or standing in groups at the lake's edge. Another group has started a game of pick-up basketball at the courts on shore, and I head in that direction as Jamie gives me a nod and heads toward the dock. A ball comes flying toward me and I snag it one-handed. I've been able to palm a basketball since I was fifteen.

I team up with a couple other guys I've met before and we start a game. The weight of the ball in my hands is familiar and welcome, although it also brings me straight back to a memory of Luke.

He was a natural athlete, and we used to play one on one together all the time. He would have beaten me every single game if we'd been the same age. I feel the familiar twinge in my chest. Luke will never be my age; and we'll never get the chance to know how good he could have been. I pull my head back into the game. Now isn't the time. I need to get it together.

Ten minutes later and there is a lull in the game. I wipe my face with my sleeve and dribble between my legs, buying time. A flash of blue catches my eye—the redhead and her brunette friend are laying out their beach towels. I watch as the redhead starts to smear sunscreen on the brunette. Do I even know her name? Absentmindedly, I hold the ball over the head of another counselor and realize I don't. Ms. Nancy said it at orientation, I think, but I've lost it since then. Why do I even care? I'm not sure. Before she turned away from me in the mess hall, her eyes locked with mine. They were some kind of blue, but not. Fuck, I don't know. They were darker, like storm clouds or something. I want to see them again. I toss the ball to another counselor and wave someone else into the game. I yanked my shirt off at the beginning of the game and now I'm just in my swim trunks. I head toward the dock, jump onto its planks, and stroll down toward the water. Jamie is standing on the edge chatting with a few counselors I recognize from last year. The redhead and the brunette are lying on their towels just a few feet past him on the dock's edge.

I step behind Jamie and, in one quick move, shove him off the pier. He falls in exactly the way I'd hoped, with a gigantic splash and a shriek like a four-year-old girl. I throw my head back, laughing so hard I think I might bust a rib, and his arm snakes out from the green water of the lake and wraps around my ankle.

"Oh, shit," I mutter, but it's too late and before I can pull my foot away I'm tumbling off the pier and into the cool water. It might be summer, but Saranac Lake still holds the chill of winter. I pop up, spluttering, and of course, Jamie is already twenty feet from me. Fuck, I think as I tread water. Jamie really must be half-fish. He pops up again six inches away from me, and before he can speak I dunk him, laughing so hard I think I might drown. I swim over to the pier and haul myself back up before Jamie can grab me again, and then reach a hand down for him. He grabs it and I yank him out of the water.

"Thanks for that, asshole," he says good-naturedly.

"Anytime," I answer, but I'm distracted by an event taking place behind us. The redheaded girl is talking to the brunette animatedly, waving her arms in the air and glancing back at me every few seconds. I grin in their direction. Sexy Redhead grins back and even gives me a little wave. The brunette glares and turns her head away from me. Well, well, I think. The kitten has claws.

CHAPTER 4
rachel

Stupid flipping show-off. Irritated, but not really understanding why, I brush the water that splashed Lexi and me when that idiot jumped in. Lexi continues gabbing in my ear about him.

"Did you *see* him, Rach? My God, when he popped back up out of the water I just about fainted. Did you see his abs? He has, like, a six pack."

I make a serious effort not to grit my teeth.

"He is just too melt-in-your-mouth gorgeous."

A headache begins to pound at the base of my temples.

"Did you see him look over at us? It was like he wanted us to be watching."

"I'm sure he did want us to be watching. It seemed like he wanted everyone to be watching."

Arrogant bastard.

I saw the way he looked at me in the mess hall. He has dark eyes that draw you in with a glance, dark hair to match, and broad shoulders. His eyes drifted over Lexi like she was a roast chicken he was considering for dinner and then they flicked to me. They were intense, focused, and I felt as though he were touching me even though he was a row of chairs away. Heat flushed my cheeks and my breathing started to escalate, and I broke our gaze. I don't know why he had the ability to do that to me with a look, but I didn't like it. He's obviously a guy who's used to getting what he wants, used to having girls like Lexi fawn all over him. That's not the kind of girl I am.

"He's coming over here," Lexi hisses in my ear. "Look!"

I straighten and, sure enough, here comes Mr. Melt-In-Your-Mouth Gorgeous. Lexi flips her silky hair over her shoulder and jumps off of her towel. I get up too, but fold my arms.

"Hey, Otter Tails," he says, as he waltzes up to us with a slow grin.

"Hey, yourself," chirps Lexi. She twirls her hair around her finger. I roll my eyes.

"I don't think I've met you two yet. I'm Shawn. I'm from Vermont. I like hamburgers and long walks on the beach."

I think Lexi is about to faint.

"I'm Lexi," she purrs, reaching out to grab his hand and hold it for a few seconds too long.

"Is that an accent I hear?"

"I'm a Texas girl."

"I could listen to you talk all day."

He smiles at her, letting his dark eyes flick over her body, which is perfectly displayed in a red bikini.

"And who's your friend?" he asks quietly, glancing at me.

His eyes go dark and intense and I feel my breath catch, entirely against my will.

"Rachel," I murmur. "I'm Rachel."

"Shawn," he says, extending a hand. I eye it for a second before taking it reluctantly His palm engulfs mine, his fingers long and capable. I can feel calluses on the tips of his fingers.

"Are you a musician?" I ask without thinking.

"Yes," he says, releasing my hand. "I'm here for sax, but I play the guitar and a little piano, too."

"That's really impressive," simpers Lexi, and I bite my cheek to keep from laughing. She has the goofiest grin on her face, and it's kind of cute even in its obviousness.

"What about you two?" asks Shawn.

"Dance," says Lexi, as though she needs to. Her body is long and graceful, speaking for itself.

"Poetry," I say.

"Oh, really? I love poetry."

"Seriously?" I know he can hear the dubious edge in my voice, but I haven't met too many teenage boys who are interested in poetry. He grins, acknowledging my doubt.

"Yeah," he says, and it rings as honest, to me. "My mother loves it; she used to read it to us before bed."

His expression darkens, just briefly, and I frown in confusion.

"That's nice," I say quietly. "My mom hates it."

Shawn laughs.

"She didn't read you poetry before bed?" he asks, teasing.

"She was never home when I went to bed," I answer honestly, and I immediately want to clap a hand over my own mouth. Shawn and Lexi are both looking at me questioningly, and I continue before I have a chance to think.

"I mean, because she was always at some event or other," I lie. "My nanny read to me every night, of course, but my mom couldn't always be there."

"She's from Manhattan," Lexi interjects, trying to regain his attention. "Upper East Side, right, Rach?"

"Oh, really?" Shawn asks, his eyes piercing mine. "High society New York?" The question is asked teasingly, but I lift my chin and nod, smiling back at him.

"Are you scared to get a little wet, New York?"

Shawn asks me. "You and Lexi are the only dry ones left on the dock."

Lexi and I lock eyes, and it's like an identical current flows through both our brains at the same time. Before Shawn can move, Lexi is pushing him from behind at the same moment I grab his arm and try to yank him in front of the water. He loses his footing in surprise, but his hand wraps around my forearm and even as I scramble backward I know I'm no match for him. We both hit the water with a splash, disappearing into a cool green world. As I kick my way back to the surface, I feel a graze of his hand across my lower back. I emerge gasping, and see his head pop up a second later. For a second we just stare at each other, and then a giggle escapes my lips. Shawn grins in response, treading water, and I grope my way back to the dock and hang onto the rough boards, choking with laughter.

"I'm sorry," Shawn says, swimming over. "I didn't mean to pull you in."

"I probably deserved it," I say, and he smiles before hauling himself out and reaching a hand down for me. He yanks me back onto the dock, and the force of it sends me flying into his chest.

Through the blur of water in my eyes I can see his white grin, and his strong chest so close to mine. Lexi was right: he definitely has a six-pack. His skin is warm beneath the water's chill, so warm it begins to heat my chilled skin in the instant we connect. We lock eyes, so close that all he'd have to do to kiss me would be to move an inch toward me. His skin is slick and wet, sliding against mine, and I feel the strangest urge to run my hands up his muscled shoulders and into his hair. I can already feel my cheeks turning red, and I finally pull away. We eye each other for another heated second, and then the other voices on the dock break the moment. I tuck a piece of my wet hair behind my ear, trying to look casual. Shawn looks calm and cool, and I wonder if I'm the only one so affected by what just happened, but then I notice the tenseness in his jaw.

"Call it even?" says Shawn. His chest is rising and falling rapidly. I resist the urge to reach out and feel how fast his heart is beating.

"Sure," I acquiesce.

"Hope you're not mad, Shawn," says Lexi brightly, stepping up behind me, but I catch the edge in her voice. Her gaze is flicking from Shawn to me and back again, her hands on her hips.

Shawn quickly turns his attention toward her, breaking the lingering connection between us.

"Are you guys competing in the volleyball tournament tomorrow?" Shawn is asking Lexi. "It's usually really fun, and a great way to get to know everyone."

"You any good at beach volleyball, Rachel?" Lexi asks.

I shrug, in the process of wringing out my wet hair. Actually, I am not completely terrible at sports. I took advanced conditioning instead of regular physical education in high school. I still might trip over my own feet at any given second, but I'm reasonably competent.

"We're in," says Lexi, grinning at Shawn.

"Great," he says. "I'll be looking forward to seeing both of you in the lineup."

He turns to me as I give up and pull my wet hair into a ponytail.

"Rachel, you're a little wet," he says.

I stick my tongue out at him as he walks away, his broad shoulders covered in droplets of water that cling to his muscles, still laughing that laugh that somehow makes me smile every time.

CHAPTER 5
rachel

The freezing water of the pitifully small shower-head is doing little to cool my heated skin. I sigh, grab more shampoo, and scrub harder. I need to be out in a few minutes to head to the mess hall for dinner. My stomach growls as I scrub my scalp; I'm starving. I think that all this fresh air is doing something to my system.

Maybe something else is messing with your system, my subconscious whispers. *And maybe it has nothing to do with the air.*

My thoughts immediately stray back to Shawn, and the heat begins to spread to my cheeks despite the water's chill. I remember the way my heart was pounding when he pulled me against him. I grab face wash and try to banish the images, but they keep rolling through my head like a slideshow I can't turn off. There is a knock on the door.

"Rachel? Are you coming out soon? Mess is in twenty minutes."

"Almost done," I call back.

I saw the look on Lexi's face after our impromptu water fight. But when Shawn invited her—well, us— to the volleyball tournament, I think she got over it. She's probably looking forward to the cute little bikini she's going to wear while we play. I look down at my body. Pale skin, freckles, legs too long for my five-foot-three frame. My hair is thick and hangs nearly to my waist, but it's a plain dark brown. Lexi looks like a bird of paradise with her red hair and green eyes, and I'm the gray moth she has for dinner. I towel-dry my hair and leave it down to dry straight as I hurry back into shorts and a camp sweatshirt. I pull on my old white Converses and dart back into the room I am sharing with Lexi. The cabin's main room is filled with sets of bunk beds—six in all, one bed for each of the twelve girls who will be a part of the Otter Tail Cabin. Each bunk bed is covered with a green blanket that has a huge maple leaf embroidered on the front. Lexi and I share a private room just off of the main one. There is a big window and another door that opens directly outside, and we have our own bathroom separate from the campers, which is nice. As soon as I pull my shoes on, Lexi heads out the door and I follow.

My back pocket buzzes suddenly as we walk toward the mess hall. I reach down and pull out my phone and see my mom's name. I sigh. I might as well answer it now, or she'll just leave me a twenty-minute voicemail complaining about it.

"Hi, Mom," I say. Lexi gives me a questioning look and I wave her forward, indicating she should head to mess without me.

"Mercedes! Hi, baby."

I wince as she says my name. It's almost painful to hear it now. It brings back stinging memories of being taunted as I walked through the halls of my high school, hearing it snickered behind girls' hands.

I went to a private high school that I was accepted to on scholarship, since we could never afford it otherwise. It was mostly full of privileged kids from wealthy, educated families. I didn't exactly fit in. I jolt back to reality as my mom says my name again.

"Mom, don't call me that," I hiss. "It's Rachel, now. I told you that before I left."

"Right," she sighs. "Sorry. I don't know why you'd want to change a perfectly beautiful name like Mercedes, anyway. How are you, sweetie?"

I ignore her comment.

"I'm fine," I continue, "It's been a busy day but I'm having a good time. I told you, you didn't need to call me all the time."

"How's it all going?" she asks, and I'm not sure she's even listening to me.

"Great, really great actually. I just-

"Honey, I met the greatest guy. You would just love him."

I'm used to her lightning-fast subject changes.

"I thought you were dating the guy you met at

the restaurant? You were going on a date with him just the other night."

"Oh, he was such a bore. Very corporate. You know, suit and tie and everything."

I roll my eyes toward the heavens.

"I thought you also said he was very nice."

"Well, so is Steve. He's from Bali. He's staying at the apartment until he finds a place."

I can already feel the headache coming on.

"Mom, do you really think that's the best decision? You barely know the guy."

I hear my mom breathe a huge sigh of annoyance into the phone.

"Darling, you really can be such a buzz kill. I'm only having a little fun."

But you always make me pick up the pieces. I'm always the one that has to be responsible.

"Yeah, Mom, I know. You always are."

"Well, I called to talk, but if you're going to be sarcastic just call me when you're in a better mood."

"I'm not in a mood. You called me to ask how I was and all we've talked about is you."

She sighs again, and I hear a deep voice in the background.

"I have to go, sweetie. I'll call you again soon."

I hear a click and then the hum of a dead line. I stop in the middle of the pathway and watch Lexi's red hair like a beacon a few yards ahead of me. The air is cooling as the sun falls, and I swear I can smell the leaves floating in the chilled air. I'm suddenly not hungry anymore.

CHAPTER 6
rachel

"**W**hat's up with you?" Lexi asks with her mouth full of carrot. Somehow, she still manages to look like an adorable pixie even with her mouth full.

"Huh?"

"You're barely eating anything."

"I'm on a health kick," I say dully.

"A health kick of . . . " she picks a piece of broccoli off of my almost empty plate and drops it again.

"My mom called," I sigh. "We don't always get along."

"Oh, you're not alone, girlfriend."

Lexi leans forward on the long bench of the mess

hall, speaking up so I can hear her amidst the background noise.

"My mom is always on my back about everything. And I mean *everything.*" She taps her bubble-gum pink nails on the table. I hide my chewed fingernails in my lap.

"She's always wanting me to cook dinner for everyone, to clean my room, to be home early. And I'm like, Mama, I can't do everything, okay? I have my own life too."

In my head I'm seeing flashes of my life, the apartment that my mom and I share. There is a pile of dishes in the cracked sink because my mom came home late and left them there. My mom has never asked me to make dinner. I make it for myself or for both of us because if I didn't, I wouldn't eat. The last time my mom cooked me something was when I was too little to reach the microwave and I'm pretty sure it was still a frozen corndog.

"What does your mom nag you about?" asks Lexi.

I snap out of it. "Um . . . " What can I say? That I'm actually the one who nags her? That our tiny apartment would be infested with cockroaches by now if it weren't for me cleaning it? That I'm used to sitting at home by myself, finishing my homework, and going to bed without ever seeing her?

"She's just always wanting me to keep my room clean," I invent wildly. "And we already have the housekeeper for that, so I just don't know why it's a big deal."

"Us, too," says Lexi, and my stomach drops as I realize she isn't lying. "Heidi comes twice a week."

"We have a live-in maid," I say. "The house is just too big."

My heart hammers against my ribs, but I can't seem to stop the words from flooding out.

"My mom and I live on the Upper East Side, like I told you earlier," I continue, "in a brownstone, but really we're only there for part of the year. The rest of the time we're at our vacation home in the Hamptons or Los Angeles."

I'm spilling out the exact words I've heard from girls in my classes over the years of high school, harbored from day after day of sitting in the back of a classroom listening to them talk about vacations in Bora Bora, the cabin in Aspen. Lexi is all ears.

"Oh, that sounds just divine. I've been asking Daddy to let us get a lake house near Tahoe for *years* now. We always ski there in the winter anyway." Her eyes sharpen suddenly, like a cat's.

"What does your father do?"

"Oh, he owns an international engineering company. He's never home, he travels for most of the year."

"You're lucky," Lexi sighs as she twists spaghetti around her fork. "My dad is in local real estate. He's always home to bug me about something."

She turns back to her food, and I try to swallow the lump in my throat as I wonder what it would be like to have your dad there every day when you got home.

That night, I am sitting on my bed with my journal when Lexi comes in from the bathroom.

"What is that?" she asks, pulling the covers of her bed back.

"My journal," I say. "I take it with me everywhere."

"You Poetry people," says Lexi. "I don't know how you do it." She smiles at me, still eyeing my journal as she lies down with a sigh. I smile back, but when she falls asleep, I sneak out of the cabin. I jump over the squeaky boards of the deck and sit on the porch railing, looking out into the darkness. The cabins on either side of ours are quiet, but the night is full of life. I can hear countless insects chirping, buzzing, and humming. Lightning bugs hover dizzily, floating in the darkness, and I can see shadows of bats swooping in to catch their dinner. A breeze blows my hair over my shoulders, and I hear an owl hoot in the distance, invisible among the trees. I pull out my journal and set it on my lap. It is faded and worn, the leather cover peeling on the edges. I open it and write sideways on the page, ignoring the darkness and the scrawl, just trying to get the words out of me and into the world:

A melting moon, yellow in the sky

And your footsteps glowing against the dark, leading me here

Where would I be without you here? Where would I be without you?

Who am I?

The question comes unbidden to the page as I hear the hoot of another owl. My pen stills as I roll the question around in my mind, in my heart, but the answer remains in the shadows.

CHAPTER 7
shawn

I wake in the morning and think of Luke as soon as I open my eyes like I always do when I'm here. Something about the piney smell of the cabin and the sound of feet stomping in the other room brings him back, and for a second it's as though he's there in the room with me. He was in another cabin with kids his age, but he would still sneak over in the mornings just to bug me. I've still never seen a kid so happy to wake up as Luke was. He was always ready to start another day, look for another adventure.

"Get up, Shawn," he would say, pulling on my shoulder. "Come on!"

How many times did I groan and roll over

for five more minutes? How many hours did I waste?

"Come on, Shawn," says Jamie. "It's time for breakfast."

I let the memory slide from my mind and roll out of bed to yank on my shoes.

At mess, everyone is crowded around the sign-up table for the volleyball tournament. I can see Rachel sitting at her table, eating rolled-up pancakes with chocolate syrup inside. I grin. She has a sweet tooth.

The redhead walks up, giving me a huge smile. What the hell is her name again? Laura, no . . . shit, Lexi. I keep forgetting, even though we just met yesterday.

"I hope you still have room for me and Rachel," she says, bending down to sign their names. She leans on her elbows toward me, giving me a nice shot practically all the way down her top. Her bra is hot pink. I flick my eyes down her shirt for just longer than an instant before meeting her gaze and giving her a slow smile. She leans a little further forward, so our lips are just inches away. My hands flex on my thighs. She's a little tease, but she's got the body and the face to pull it off.

"I'm sure we'll be able to slide you in. Somewhere," I murmur. I grin at her and she stands up slowly, looking satisfied. Her eyes gleam like a tiger's, cunning and calculated.

"That's just what a girl likes to hear," she purrs. She slides a hand through her hair in a way that makes me think about how it would feel to run my hands through it, and then turns and walks away from the table, hips swinging. She's rolled her camp shorts up a few times so I can see the curve of her ass peeking under the bottom.

"Damn," murmurs Jamie. "What's her name again?"

I think he might have actually gone pale in the thirty seconds she was at the table. I slap him on the back.

"It's Laura. Fuck, no, it's Lexi," I say. "And she sure knows what she's doing."

"How do you forget the name of a girl like that? She looked at you like you were dinner."

"I'm thinking more along the lines of dessert."

"How do you do it, man? The women flock to you in herds. It's unfair."

I snort, trying not to choke on the pancake currently in my mouth.

I glance over at Lexi's table again as they gather their trays and leave. As Rachel heads toward the door I notice circles under her eyes. I wonder briefly if she's not sleeping well. I wonder why her name has stuck in my mind since the moment I first heard it.

CHAPTER 8
shawn

By noon, the sun is beating on my shoulders with such intensity that I can feel the beads of sweat dripping down my back. I'm covered in sand and I leap up to spike another ball that crosses the net, enjoying the loud slap it makes against my hand. The ball hits the sand on the opposite side as the two guys we're playing both dive for it.

"That's game!" I yell. Jamie and I high five and then walk around to shake hands with the guys. Swimming has given Jamie some strong lungs; he never seems winded. He can hold his breath for almost two minutes. I never see him even breathing hard. He is, however, starting to resemble a lobster.

"Jesus, man," I say, poking his bony shoulder. The skin turns an angry pink again almost immediately. Jamie winces.

"I know, I know," he says. "I'm frying like a burger on a grill."

"I have sunscreen," I hear, and I turn to see Rachel heading toward us. She's wearing a gold bikini top that brings out the blue in her eyes. They're really more gray, I realize all over again as I study her. Like rainclouds. She glares at me pointedly, her cheeks turning pink from my scrutiny, but I don't turn away. It's cute when she's angry.

"Oh, dear God," moans Jamie as she spreads lotion on his cherry-red shoulders. "You're an angel."

She smiles, spreading the lotion, and a trickle of irritation spreads through my veins. She still has ink covering the edge of her left arm, but it's faded, like she tried to wash it off and gave up.

"My mom is pale, like me," she says. "She would be burnt every single day in the summer if it weren't for me." She spins the cap back on the bottle of lotion.

"What about me?" I spread my arms and look down at myself. Rachel steps back and folds her arms, cocking her hip out and frowning at me. Her hair falls into her eyes and she looks ridiculously sexy, standing there like that.

"Turn around," she says.

I'm surprised. I expected her to refuse. But I do as she asks, jumping a little when her fingers first find my skin. She spreads the lotion, reaching a little to get the top of my shoulders.

"Thanks," I say, turning back around.

She gives me a hesitant smile and I grin back at her as her eyes flick over me. I stand there, unabashedly doing the same back to her. Her cheeks turn pink all over again and I like knowing I affect her even though she tries to act otherwise.

"Where are you guys at on the roster?" I ask.

"We're playing Carlos and Mary Beth next," she says.

"Are you two any good?"

Her eyes flash, and her lips curve up on one side. Damn.

"We're not bad," she says.

"Will you make it to the end?"

"Why?"

"Because we will. And I want to play you."

"Why?"

"So many questions."

"I was just wondering."

"Well, you can keep wondering. I'll see you in the playoffs."

I give her a final grin and turn back toward the net. This should be interesting.

CHAPTER 9
shawn

For such a little thing, she's not bad at volleyball. As Jamie and I are shaking hands with the last team we beat, I glance over at the adjacent nets where she and Lexi are matched up against two other counselors. She's light on her feet, quick to get up from the sand, and she has a good sense of where the ball is going. Lexi is a much flashier player, quicker and more explosive, but Rachel is steady. They make a good team.

The call of a megaphone rings out suddenly, announcing the final playoff game.

"That's us," Jamie says. "Do you think the girls won their last game, too?"

Even as he asks it, the two are walking toward the net. Jamie rubs a hand over the back of his head and cracks his knuckles.

"Nervous?" I ask.

"No way," he says.

"Maybe we should get you an icepack for those shoulders."

"Fuck you, man."

We walk up to the girls to shake hands before the game starts. Lexi squeezes mine, brushing her thumb over the top of my hand, but Rachel drops it almost as soon as we've touched. Her skin is surprisingly cool and smooth, despite how hard I've seen her playing. The sun is beginning to set over the lake.

"Well, this is romantic," I say, and Lexi giggles in a high voice. Rachel turns and stares at the sky. When she turns back toward us, her eyes are pale gray in the light, the orange in the sky bringing out the blue. For once, I don't tease her. I just look her over for a few seconds while the referee explains the rules and wishes us a good game. She looks back at me, standing very still, cheeks flushed from the games, and covered in sand. I think we both feel what's happening, but at the same time, we both know that personal relationships between counselors are discouraged throughout camp's duration. Rachel tilts her head a little to the left, and finally I smile. She gives me a wide smile in return, and I'm surprised at how perfect it is.

"What do you say we make this a little . . . more interesting?" says Lexi, as the referee finishes up.

"I'm all ears," says Jamie.

I nod. "What did you have in mind?"

"Whoever loses the game pays a forfeit," says Lexi. "A forfeit of the winner's choice."

Rachel's eyes are wide, although whether it's from excitement or nervousness I can't quite tell.

"Excellent," I say. I love a challenge.

"Yeah, I'm all for it," says Jamie. "We can decide on the terms when we win."

"Oh, we'll see about that," says Lexi. "Rach, are you in?"

Rachel just shrugs and nods. "Yeah, sure. Whatever."

We turn and walk to our side of the net. I stretch out, again, the muscles I've used all day feeling tense. There is an ache in one of my shoulders, and my legs are slower than they were this morning. Rachel winces as she stretches out her calves and I know she's starting to get stiff, too. Lexi casually turns her backside toward us, bending down to stretch her hamstrings. She moves into a runner's lunge, still with her back toward us, and shoots me a smile. Jamie has stopped warming up altogether and is just standing with his mouth open like a jackass. Lexi stands up and links arms with Rachel, talking strategy, and I head over to Jamie.

"Pull it together, man," I say, slapping him on the back.

"Ow," is all he says, when I accidentally hit his sunburn.

"It's game time, bro. It's time to bring the pain."

"Uh huh." He shakes his head, snapping out of his sexual coma.

"I'm in it, man. I'm ready. Let's do this."

We high five again and line up as Lexi tosses the ball in the air.

At first, I think we will beat them easily. How could we not? We outweigh each girl by at least sixty pounds, and we have way more muscle mass. But Lexi has a mean spike, and Rachel is as steady as a lake. Even when she starts to sweat, hair coming loose from her ponytail and sticking to her face, she never fades. She's always there to back up Lexi, always there to just barely get under a ball and pop up again, covered in sand. I'm impressed, honestly. We've had a couple mistakes, too, once when Lexi's bikini top started to come undone and Jamie got distracted and took a ball to the face, and again when the last rays of sunlight got into my eyes and I missed a ball I should have gotten. I'm sweating, breathing hard, and glad this is the last game of the day. But I enjoy watching Rachel, keeping an eye on her even as I run over the sand. Lexi keeps jumping in my line of vision, trying to get my attention, and I admit I appreciate her chest bouncing around in that bikini top, but I can't help but keep my eye on Rachel. She's so understated compared to Lexi, and it's refreshing. I already know what Lexi's about. She lays every card she has right on the table as soon as you meet her. But Rachel is a mystery to me.

It's final point, and we're serving. *Please, God,* I think. *Please let Jamie not notice that Lexi is bending over with her hands on her knees again.* I crouch into a squat as he slaps the ball behind me and it soars over the net, but Rachel is already on one knee in the sand, bumping it over to Lexi. Lexi spikes it just as Jamie and I head for where it crosses the net, but Jamie slams into me and we roll into a heap in the sand. There is cheering and clapping from the crowd, almost everyone stayed to watch the final match. I pull Jamie from the sand, and he shakes his head and gives me a shrug as if to say, *Oh well.* I grin at him, realizing this means that we'll have to pay a forfeit to the girls. I'm normally a sore loser, but that at least is a bit of a balm. We walk up to the girls to shake hands again.

"Congratulations, ladies," I say. Lexi is bouncing up and down, practically rubbing her hands together in anticipation. Rachel has her fists on her hips. A bead of sweat trickles down the side of her neck, and my throat tightens. Jamie and I grab our bags and I pull my camp shirt over my head, enjoying the breeze that starts to dry the sweat from my body. The four of us start walking down the path toward the mess hall. Jamie and Lexi are both chattering but Rachel and I are quiet, walking beside each other. I snap back to attention as I hear my name come out of Lexi's mouth.

"And for my forfeit, I choose . . . Shawn," she says. Shocker.

"Looks like you're stuck with me," says Jamie to Rachel. She smiles at him.

"I hope you don't mind," she says, and Jamie shakes his head and they start discussing his forfeit. I am irrationally irritated that Jamie will now get to spend some time with Rachel. More than that, he'll be doing something for her. I don't want someone else doing things for her. Lexi strides up next to me, and I fight the irritation. Lexi is cute, after all. She links her arm through mine and smiles up at me.

"I've got big plans for you," she says, giving me a wide smile. An image of a piranha pops into my mind.

"I'll just bet you do," I say. In the shadows, Rachel scowls.

CHAPTER 10
shawn

The next day, morning rolls around to find me facedown on my bed. I'm due to meet Lexi in an hour and I do not want to go. With the way she was hanging on my arm and laughing in my ear last night, I can't imagine she has anything planned for me that I'd even remotely want to do. But I made a bet, and I lost. I'll hold up my end even if it means spending an early hour or two before orientation being her slave. Sighing, I throw open my back door and head toward the Otter Tail cabin. It might be early, but sunlight is already streaming in through the trees and burning off the morning chill. I stroll even more slowly, buying myself a few more minutes of peace. I take a shortcut off the trail that I know will let me out somewhere around the backside of the Otter Tail cabin. Its one of the perks of being a returning counselor, I know the grounds inside and out. I've already run into a new girl who asks me for directions every single time I see her. She's perpetually lost, and every time I try to point her in the right direction I'm unsure as to whether she ever finds her way or just keeps wandering aimlessly. She'll figure it out, though. Everyone does eventually.

I head for a break in the trees and, sure enough, my little trek has led me straight to the back of the cabin. Everything is so quiet before the campers get here. I'm going to miss the peace, but I like it better when everything is noisy and chaotic. As I near the back door, I hear a rustle in the high grass surrounding the cabin. I step forward carefully, hoping not to step on some animal hiding in the grass. I hear another rustle and stop in my tracks.

"Shawn?"

I nearly jump out of my skin, but I'm just thankful I didn't shriek and embarrass myself further.

Rachel pokes her head up from her spot in the grass, biting back a smile. I take a few steps forward and can see where Rachel has laid a blanket in the grass. She is sitting cross-legged, her hair pulled back from her face, and her journal or some book is in her lap. She is bright-eyed and smiling at me, as early as it is.

"Hi," I say finally, stepping onto the edge of the grass she's flattened down with her blanket. "I didn't, uh . . . see you there."

"I was hiding," she says, and she gives me a wide smile. "I mean, just taking a minute to write before the day started. Are you here to see Lexi?"

"Yeah, I guess," I answer, and she smiles at me again but it's tinged with sadness. She looks down at the book in her hands, tracing the worn material.

"Can I stay here with you?" I ask suddenly, feeling like a seven-year-old boy. "Just for a while," I finish sheepishly, and Rachel laughs.

"Yeah," she shrugs. "Sure. I'm not doing anything very interesting out here."

She shifts over on the blanket, making room for me, and I sit down beside her. Her thigh brushes against mine and I swallow, hard. Her face is flushed and I'm not sure if it's from the heat or from me sitting so close, but more and more I hope it's the latter. She reaches up to tuck a lock of hair behind her ear and I find myself watching her.

"So, are we just going to pretend that you didn't scream like a little girl when I scared you?" says Rachel, and I burst out laughing.

"Just when I was starting to think how sweet you are," I say, and Rachel snorts. "And for the record, I did not scream. I jumped, a little, because I was prepared to leap into action."

Rachel rolls her eyes.

"What are you doing out here, anyway?" I ask.

"Just writing," she says. "I wanted to come out and sit in the sun."

"I'd think a city girl like you would be scared of the bears and the bugs," I tease, and she shoves me playfully.

"No way," she says quietly. "I love this. It's a million times better than smog."

"Can't argue there," I answer, and we sit in silence for a moment. I am becoming more and more aware of how close she is, the way the sun is warming her skin. Every time she shifts on the blanket I want to lay her down and . . .

"Hey, guys," says a voice on the steps, and I pop out of the grass.

"I thought I heard your voice, Shawn," says Lexi. She walks down the steps and toward Rachel and I with a smile like a crocodile, and I'm not sure which one of us is the fish she's about to eat.

I don't want her asking what Rachel and I were doing together, so my only choice is to distract her.

"I'm here to pay my forfeit," I say, grinning at Lexi, and her face lights up.

"Oh, really," she purrs, grabbing the front of my shirt. "We'll just have to see what we can come up with for you."

"Sounds great," I say, smiling into her eyes. I'm hyper-aware of Rachel's presence at my back and the way her body stiffened when Lexi arrived. I don't know why I'm so drawn to Rachel instead of Lexi, and I almost wish it were the other way around. There's a lot I don't know about Rachel; she's layered, and what you see is just a piece of who she is. Lexi is the complete opposite. She grabs the bag she left sitting on the bottom of the steps and heads back to me.

"Are you ready?" she says. "I have quite the morning planned for you."

Rachel storms ahead of us, and all I can do is nod and smile back.

"I'm ready," I say, but all I'm thinking about is Rachel's laugh this morning and the way her skin felt when it brushed against mine.

Sunlight is streaming through the open window in my room in full force by the time I'm finished. We have half an hour before orientation stuff begins, and I'm spending it lying facedown on my bed. I've already spent my morning running around after Lexi.

Jamie opens the door to our room and I hear him start to laugh.

"There you are. What are you doing? I thought you'd be off doing whatever Lexi wanted."

I groan and roll over, linking my hands behind my head.

"That's what I did," I said. "She basically just had me follow her everywhere. Her and Rachel went swimming, and I had to rub sunscreen on her. She asked me to rub her feet at one point and I flat out refused."

Jamie is grinning so widely it looks like his face might split in half.

"Well, well, well. How the tables have turned."

I frown and sit up. "How so?"

"You had to wait hand and foot on miss sassy pants. You know what Rachel wants?"

I shake my head, although I'm hoping it's not rubbing lotion on her back.

"Piano lessons."

"Seriously?"

"Yeah. She's always wanted to learn, I guess.

There's not much I can do for her in one lesson, but I'm supposed to help her out this afternoon during our break."

"You lucky bastard."

"I know."

In the mess hall a half hour later, I've just finished loading up a plate of mashed potatoes and gravy with ham when Lexi pops up next to me.

"Hi, Shawn," she says. Jamie, standing next to me in the line, does a double take and heads for the table, mumbling something about saving me a seat. Traitor.

"Hi, Lexi," I say, equally casual. "What can I do for you?"

"Well, I was a little sad that our deal ended."

"Oh, me too. Seriously. I'm bummed about it."

"If there's anything you can think of that I could give you in return . . . " she trails off. "Don't be afraid to ask."

She looks up at me, and I can't help but smile. She's a giant pain in the ass, and I'd cut my left arm off before I'd date her, but she has her cute moments. She walks back toward her table and I'm passing her when Rachel catches my eye. She's staring at me with a look that's somewhere between a scowl and something I can't quite place. I give her a smile as I walk by, just to see what she'll do. She folds her arms, frowning at me, and I wink at her. She rolls her eyes at me, but the corners of her mouth start to curve up. She turns back to her table, but not before I see the flush of color in her cheeks. Lexi can flirt with me all she wants, I even enjoy it some of the time, but nothing she's done so far has come close to the twist in my stomach Rachel gives me with a blush.

CHAPTER 11
rachel

I can't write. I can't write *anything*. I stare down at the blank page in front of me, willing something to come. My hand remains motionless. I'm still sitting with my journal in my hands on the blue Otter Tail comforter that covers my tiny twin bed when Lexi throws the door open and stomps in. I lost track of her sometime after Ms. Nancy released us for our afternoon break. Automatically, I close my journal and double-check the silver lock that adorns the front. It only opens with the key I always have on a band around my wrist.

"He's doing this to me on purpose," Lexi says, throwing herself facedown onto her bed with a dramatic thump and sigh.

"He flirts with me, alright," she continues, rolling over to face me, and I resign myself to listening. "He flirts with me, and he touches me—"

"He touches you?" Suddenly, I am all ears.

"Not like that," she sighs. "I just mean little ones. He'll touch my hand or my waist or even my hair, but he never pulls me close."

She pouts.

"I don't know why. I've given him every possible opportunity."

I resist the urge to roll my eyes. The whole camp has noticed Lexi's preoccupation with Shawn. I walked past a table at mess this morning and heard two girls whispering about it.

Who does she think she is, anyway? Throwing herself at him like that.

But he flirts back with her. I think he's just leading her on.

I cringed and kept walking. Besides, I think Lexi knows she's making a stir and just doesn't care. I have to admire her for that.

"What's up with you two, anyway?" Lexi asks

suddenly. She is sitting up on her bed, looking at me with narrowed green eyes. "I saw you rubbing lotion on him yesterday. And then you two were together randomly this morning."

I freeze, desperately trying to seem casual. Is what's happening between us that obvious?

"Nothing," I say finally. "Nothing is going on."

I flash back to this morning, the way my stomach cartwheeled when I saw Shawn walking toward the cabin. I didn't mean to scare him; I meant to say something to let him know I was there, but just seeing him tied my tongue into knots.

"Are you sure?" Lexi asks.

She's looking at me like a cat about to pounce. I'm the mouse.

"Yeah," I say, meeting her eyes. "I have so many guys to deal with back home that I'm really not looking to add one to the list."

"Oh, really?" says Lexi, looking interested.

"Yeah," I say, winding my fingers in my hair. I invent some wild story about the guy who took me on his yacht, another who invited me on his private jet to see an opera. Lexi nods and listens intently, but there is a gleam in her eye that I don't like.

"Where did you go to high school again?" she asks.

"The Harvest Academy," I say honestly.

"A private school?" says Lexi, and I nod.

"That must have been expensive," she says shrewdly, and I nod.

"We could afford it," I lie. No way am I going to tell her I was there on scholarship, the poor girl in a sea of dollar signs.

"I have to go," I say as I stand up. "I have to go meet Jamie."

"For your piano lesson?"

I nod.

"Great," she says. "I'll see you after, then. And you're going to the bonfire tonight with me, right?"

"Yeah, sure," I say. Our campers arrive tomorrow, and I'm both excited and terrified to meet them.

I slide my journal under my pillow when it looks like Lexi is engrossed with whatever is on her phone screen. But as I head for the door, I feel her eyes on my back with every step I take.

CHAPTER 12

rachel

Jamie is already waiting for me in the music room. I felt a little stupid asking him for a piano lesson, as though I were a four-year-old, but I've always loved music and never had the opportunity to learn. I didn't have the time in my schedule to take a music class at Harvest. Jamie grins as I walk up to the building, which is settled back in the trees. It's a big room with smaller annexes for practice areas, and it has wonderful acoustics. I remember it from the tour of the grounds we took earlier in orientation.

"Hi there," he greets me. "Please don't judge my teaching skills. I'm used to little kids."

I smile. Jamie always makes me laugh. I feel very comfortable around him.

As we walk inside, Shawn comes out of one of the separate music rooms, his saxophone slung around his neck. He looks ridiculously sexy, his long fingers spread over the keys of the sax.

"Hi, Rach," he says to me. I frown at him, which feels like all I've been doing lately.

"What are you doing here?" I ask, rudely, but he just grins at me. I'm still a little offended by the way he flirted with Lexi this morning, but I'm even angrier at myself for caring. He's not mine. He can flirt with whomever he chooses. Damn him for making me want to smile even as I want to punch him in the face.

"I'm just practicing," he says. "I wanted to brush up before everyone gets here tomorrow."

"Oh."

I shouldn't care. It shouldn't matter to me that he's here at the same time we are. But I am. I'm irritated that he's standing close to me and that he smells like a mixture of sunscreen and a sexy, musky scent I can't place.

"Do you play?" he asks, gesturing to the piano.

"No," I answer. "Not at all."

"Well, you can't go wrong with Jamie as a teacher," he says easily. "He's great."

Jamie leads me to the black piano nestled in the corner and seats himself next to me, opening a beginner's book.

"Okay," he says. "Let's show you middle C."

He begins to help me pick out notes, to read the simple music in the book. I'm learning exceedingly simple material, like "Mary Had a Little Lamb," but Jamie is endlessly patient, and I'm enjoying myself. Shawn heads back into the other room—the music rooms in this building are nearly soundproof, so even though the notes barely carry to me, I find myself distracted by his playing. The way he coaxes sound out of the instrument is beautiful, and even though I know next to nothing about what he's playing, I can recognize his skill. Another new counselor walks in and I hear Shawn talking with him, showing him proper technique and giving him tips. I wouldn't have thought Shawn would have that kind of patience. I refocus, turning my mind back to the piano.

At the end of an hour, I can play "Mary Had a Little Lamb" flawlessly, as well as "Twinkle Twinkle Little Star." I'm definitely no expert, but Jamie made me feel very comfortable and I enjoyed myself, despite Shawn's distracting presence.

"Thank you so much for doing this," I say to Jamie. "I really appreciate it you taking the time to do this for me."

"It's no problem," he says. "I had a good time, too."

Shawn and the other counselor come out of the other room, looking over a piece of sheet music. They are still going over it, and finally I hear the other counselor thanking Shawn for his help.

"I wouldn't have thought Shawn was so patient," I say.

Jamie turns to me.

"Really? Yeah, he is. He's great with the campers, too. They idolize him."

"Why is he a counselor?"

Jamie stands next to the piano, looking down at the black and white keys.

"Uh, he had a little brother he used to come here with when they were younger. He passed away a couple of years ago."

I feel like I've just swallowed my heart and it's lost somewhere now inside my throat.

"Oh, my God," I murmur. "I had no idea."

"Yeah, he doesn't talk about it much. But he's come back to be a counselor since the year his brother passed."

"What was his name?"

"Luke."

Shawn strolls up to us, taking the saxophone off from around his neck. He takes one look at my face and groans.

"Dammit, Jamie," he starts, and Jamie is already holding up his hands and backing away.

"Man, I'm sorry," says Jamie. "She asked."

"What?" I say, turning from Shawn to Jamie and back.

"I know he told you," says Shawn impatiently. "It was written all over your face. As soon as I walked over here you looked at me like I was a stray dog someone just kicked."

I open my mouth to deny it, but it's true. And I get why he's upset. He doesn't want to be treated with pity because of his tragedy. And when I think about it, I wouldn't either.

"You're right," I say, interrupting Jamie and Shawn, who are still arguing. "It did make me see you differently. But don't worry. Those rose-colored glasses were only on for about thirty seconds."

Jamie just stares at me, but Shawn snorts out a laugh.

"I get it," I shrug. "Relax. It's like he never told me."

Jamie looks at me gratefully, and on Shawn's face I see honest relief.

"Thanks," he says quietly, with none of his usual teasing.

I nod. "Thanks again, Jamie," I say.

"No big deal," he says easily. The door opens and another counselor walks inside looking for Jamie, who steps away. Suddenly, it's just Shawn and I. There is a moment of quiet, and I twist my fingers in the hem of my tank top.

"Are you going to the bonfire tonight?" he asks. His eyes are lighter in the rays of the sun that come through the window, bringing out specks of green amid the brown. I struggle to coordinate my thoughts.

"Um, yes," I say. "Yeah, Lexi was going to drag us both down there after dinner."

"Do you like s'mores?"

"So many questions," I tease, and his face lights up with humor. "Yes, I do. I love them. And so does Lexi," I add as an afterthought, trying to at least make an attempt to bring her back into the conversation.

Shawn just nods.

"It looked like your lesson went well."

"It did," I say honestly. "I had a great time."

"Maybe you can perform 'Mary Had a Little Lamb' for the showcase," teases Shawn. The showcase is basically a big performance at the end of camp where everyone, campers and counselors, perform what they've been working on for the past two weeks. There is also a special newsletter that comes out after the showcase, displaying the best works from Poetry and Fiction. The best performers at the showcase, or the best pieces submitted to the newsletter, which is another option, are chosen. Just thinking about it ties my stomach up into knots. I'm not big on public performances. The last time I tried, I was in the fourth grade. I stood up in front of everyone at the school talent show and, almost immediately, passed out. I needed four stitches in the back of my head. Since then, I've worked through a lot of my fear, but it's still difficult for me to go on stage.

"Yeah, right," I say. "I'm scared to perform in front of everyone as it is."

"You're nervous to read one of your poems?"

"Well, yeah. Wouldn't you be?"

"I guess," he admits. "I'm not a huge writer, though. Although I did a little of it after Luke."

I can see the pain in his face, and I'm surprised he's admitting this to me.

"Writing can help a lot with tough situations," I say slowly. "It's helped me through a lot of them."

"Like what?" Shawn asks, his brow wrinkled. I know he's thinking of the fact that, according to what I've told everyone so far, I have a privileged childhood filled with everything I could ever need.

"Oh, you know," I say vaguely. "Just normal teenage stuff."

I'm thinking of the humiliation of my worn-in clothes compared to those with the means to never wear the same thing twice. Things like that shouldn't matter, but in high school, they matter a lot. It hurts just to remember. I never want Shawn to see me as that girl, to look at me the way they did.

"Right," is all he says.

"You know," I add, on a wave of inspiration, "if you ever wanted to work on poetry with me, we could do that. Outside of the time I'm working with the campers."

He is smiling, staring at me with those dark eyes, and it makes my stomach jump for no good reason.

"Yeah," he says. "That would be amazing, actually."

There is another moment of quiet, both of us looking the other over, wanting more but afraid to take the jump.

"I'll see you guys at the bonfire, then," says Shawn finally. He is still staring at me, eyes locked with mine, and I'm frozen in place.

"Yes," I say, but it comes out in a whisper. "Yes, we'll be there."

I am suddenly angry, irritated with him as I usually am. Why does he affect me this way? I didn't ask for it. I don't want it. And Lexi certainly does. I practically run from him out the door, but not before I catch the surprised look on his face. I glance behind me as I continue down the path to see Shawn through the front window standing exactly where I left him. He is still staring at me. The jump in my stomach only irritates me more.

CHAPTER 13
rachel

"**D**id you see Shawn at your lesson?" This is obviously Lexi's first question when she plops down beside me on the bench at dinner that evening. I'm eating my favorite snack—oatmeal-raisin cookies with jelly spread all over them. My journal is sitting safely next to me, the little silver lock clicked shut.

"Yeah," I answer Lexi. "He was there with Jamie."

"How did he look?"

An image of his long fingers playing over the saxophone keys jumps to mind, then his eyes in the sunlight as he smiled at me.

"I don't know," I say. "Normal."

"Right, right."

"He said he's coming to the bonfire."

"Really? Tonight?"

"Yup. That very one."

"I can't wait. I wish I could wear something besides all this stupid camp stuff."

I look down at the gray crewneck sweatshirt I pulled on before dinner. It has the camp logo on it and then an outline of a swimming otter with our cabin name on top. It's so soft inside.

"I probably won't even have time to wash my hair," she whines.

My hair is pulled up into a high ponytail, but at least it's clean. For a girl coming to camp straight from New York, I thought I'd be having more transition issues, but I'm not. I love my tiny bed with the soft cotton sheets, and the way the air smells like nothing but maple and pine. I don't want to go back to my mom's and my tiny apartment in the smog with the piles of trash on the sidewalk.

I frown. I haven't been able to write here, though, not lately. I'm going to college at a prestigious art school in Vermont next year with a great poetry program. I'm always scribbling somewhere—on my own skin half the time if I don't have my journal handy. My hand is startlingly blank now. I flip it over, but there's no text anywhere on my skin. And the side of my arm where the ink always smudges is perfectly clean. The words are there, I can hear them humming in my skull, but they won't come out. A part of me wonders if I'm the one keeping them hidden from myself, but I push the thought away.

Lexi grabs my arm, yanking me up from the table.

"Well, come on," she says impatiently. "We have to go get ready."

"We?" I say, but she is already propelling me outside.

By the time Lexi and I are heading to the bonfire, I have smudged eyeliner on my eyelids and mascara coating my unwilling lashes. Lexi chased me with lipstick for ten minutes before I finally compromised by letting her swipe some pale gloss over my lips.

"How can a rich city girl hate makeup so much?" she said, finishing up my mascara.

"I just never got that into it," I said, and that's mostly the truth. I'm guessing most girls learn about makeup from their moms, but that was never going to happen to me. My mom likes to wear her makeup heavy and dark. I can picture it now: blue or purple eye shadow, dark eyeliner, red lipstick, hair curled and piled on top of her head. She likes to show off her outfits to me before a date, circling the living room in silver heels and short skirts.

"Don't I look fabulous, baby?" she would say.

She is blonde and hazel-eyed, slim and tall. I look nothing like her. She says I take after my father, but whenever I ask about him she either changes the subject or pretends not to hear me.

Lexi loops her arm through mine, babbling to me about something, and I jolt back to the present.

"I'm so excited," Lexi whispers as we approach the crowd of counselors gathered around the fire. It's burning as high as my waist, reflecting shimmers of light onto the quiet surface of the lake behind it. I am suddenly nervous. While Lexi and I stand by the edge of the fire, the blonde I waved to at mess comes up to us.

"Hi," she says, a huge smile showing her dimples. "We talked by the dock the other day, right?"

"Yeah," I say. "Yeah, I'm Rachel."

"Julie," she says.

Before I know it, we are going on about making friendship bracelets and talking about ways to keep our young campers occupied. Lexi tugs on my sleeve. At least, I had managed to keep her from forcing me to change out of my comfy sweatshirt.

"I'm going to go and say hi to Shawn," she whispers to me. "It was nice to meet you, Julie," she says, and then she's off, her hips swaying in the firelight. She has a natural grace in her movements that I know I could never achieve in my wildest dreams. I've only known her a few days but the amount of time she spends dedicated to Dance is starting to astound me. She stretches for more than an hour in the cabin at the end of the day, or at lunch, or both. It hurts just to watch her.

Julie and I head toward the fire, grabbing

marshmallows and chocolate on the way. I glance over and see where Lexi is talking to Shawn, who is standing in a group of other people, including Jamie. Jamie sees us standing by the fire and waves at me.

"Who is that?" Julie asks.

"That's Jamie."

"He's really cute," she whispers.

"Jamie?"

I look over at the group again. Jamie is long and gangly and reminds me of a grasshopper, but he does have eyes that always smile when he smiles, and he always makes me laugh.

We walk around the fire to the boys, and I lead Julie up to Jamie. He proceeds to be as friendly as I have come to expect, immediately asking Julie questions about herself while still including me in the conversation. Out of the corner of my eye, I glimpse Shawn talking to Lexi, and I'm filled with a mixture of annoyance and something else I don't care to define. His back is to me, though, which gives me the chance to study him without him noticing, and it gives me little thrills deep in my stomach. Lexi tilts her head and touches his arm and I ball my hands into fists.

"You okay, Rachel?" says Jamie, and I jump.

"Yeah, yeah, of course," I say. "Let's make another s'more."

We move to the other side of the fire, but I can't stop watching Shawn with Lexi. His hands are shoved in his pockets, but she continues touching him casually every chance she gets. He's smiling and talking back to her, and I'm getting more and more uncomfortable. *What do I care if he talks to Lexi all night?* I ask myself. I don't. I don't care at all. But deep down, I can tell that I'm fighting a losing battle. Dammit, I do care. I don't know why, but I do, and it's getting harder and harder to act like I don't.

"I'm going to head back to my cabin," I tell Jamie and Julie.

"Are you sure?" asks Julie. "It's still pretty early."

"Yeah," I say. "I'm really tired from today."

I give each of them a hug and then stride off into the darkness. I don't want to go back to my cabin yet. I walk in the darkness, following the path by memory and the light of a huge, round moon. The sky is sapphire velvet dotted with sprinkles of lights, and creatures rustle in the bushes next to me. I did some research before camp, because even though I was ready to get out of the city, the only wild animals I had ever come into contact with were stray cats outside the apartment. I know there are rabbits and foxes hiding in the shadows, though, and I've seen the flash of an owl swooping through the dark. I wander into the clearing that leads down to the dock closest to my cabin. The huge moon reflects onto the dark surface of the water. I walk down the gently creaking planks of the dock and watch the ripples spread. I stand at the very edge and let the moonlight bathe me in a pale glow, and that's when I hear his voice.

"Rachel?"

When I left, I think a part of me hoped for him to follow, but I'm still filled with a wild mixture of emotions from watching him flirt with Lexi all night.

"What do you want?" I say quietly, even though he is still standing on the shore.

"Why did you leave?"

"Why did you?"

He takes a step onto the dock, and I take an automatic step backward.

"Why are you running from me, Rachel?"

"I'm not," I answer, but haven't I been since I met him? Aren't I still running, even now?

"You look like an angel, standing there," he says. He's about three feet in front of me now, hands shoved in his front pockets. "The moon is making you glow."

I stare at him, watching the way the shadows play over his face. Who says things like that? There is a moment of silence, unbroken except for cricket song and the lapping of lake water.

"Why are you here?" I ask.

"I saw you leave. I followed you."

"Why?"

"I think you know why."

He is grinning at me, and a part of me so badly

wants to melt in the heat of his gaze. My heart has suddenly become two sizes too big for my chest.

"No, I don't. You like Lexi."

"Lexi likes me. It's not the same thing."

"Tell that to her," I mumble, and he grins.

"I know. She, uh, comes on a little strong."

I nod, and feel a trickle of guilt. I know Lexi would give anything to be standing exactly where I am right now, but at the same time I can't make my legs move. My whole body is vibrating. He takes a step closer.

"Don't," I say.

"Don't what?" he says softly, still coming toward me.

"Just . . . wait." Is that my voice? It's breathy and low, and my blood is running through my veins like fire. I know all the reasons this needs to stop before anything really happens: the fact that counselors aren't supposed to be romantically involved, that I've always promised myself I wouldn't let myself fall for someone so dangerous. I've lived through those mistakes. Despite knowing this, here I am. I could run, but I don't.

He is so close now. He reaches out and takes my hands, tangling my fingers with his, and I stare down at them in the moonlight. His hands are huge, making mine look tiny and fragile. I try to pull away, but he just tugs me toward him, and I so badly want to step into his arms, but I am terrified beyond belief. I twist away from him, but all that happens is that he pulls me closer, holding me against his body, and I can't resist the way my head feels under his chin.

He wraps his arms around me and pulls me in, and a part of me still wants to run, but a larger part can't get my feet to move. I didn't know he was capable of making me feel so safe. The part of me that wanted to protest ebbs away.

"I have to go," I say from within the circle of his arms.

"Sure you do," he says. We stand for a few seconds, and I try to absorb what it feels like to be held against him. He pulls back so we are face to face, and his hands slide across my lower back.

"I can't," I whisper, but he just stares at me and the words float away like dandelion seeds in the wind.

"I'll let you go right now if you tell me again."

"I have to go."

He looks pained, but true to his word, he steps back from me and drops his arms.

"Do you mean that?"

There is a pause, and I can't help but smile. His mouth quirks up and he moves back to me with one slow step. He leans toward me and my heart clenches. He starts running his lips along the edge of my jaw and down my neck, and I can't fight it anymore.

"No, I don't," I whisper, and his lips are on mine, warm and soft but possessive at the same time, as though he's branding me with his mouth alone. I shiver even as heat floods my body and I throw my arms around his neck. He wraps his arms even more tightly around my waist, kissing his way down my neck, each touch soft against my skin.

And with every second that passes, I feel more and more out of control.

I pull his face back to mine and I feel him smile against my lips, but I am greedy now and I press my body harder against his. He groans, spreading his hands across my lower back and moving them forward to stroke my hipbones with his thumbs. I am up on my tiptoes, arms wrapped around his shoulders as he strokes my lower lip with his tongue, biting it gently. I know I would fall if he weren't holding me up, and I know that everything in me has been fighting against this moment, but right now I just can't bring myself to care.

I pull back, fighting to catch my breath. For a moment there's just the sound of our breathing. I glance up at him, shy for some reason, and he's staring at me in the light of the moon. I can see his chest rising and falling just as fast as mine.

"Rachel . . . " he says, just my name, and I am sure he was right all along, that it was never a trick of the moon but that my body is really glowing, drawing energy from somewhere deep inside me.

I fall back down from my tiptoes but he locks his

hands around my lower back. The cool air blowing over the lake clears my head and I know I can't stay.

"Shawn," I whisper. "I have to go."

"No," he says, pulling me back and doing delicious things to the inside of my ear.

"Yes," I say, bracing my hands against his chest. "I have to."

"When will I see you again?"

"I don't know."

"Soon?"

"I don't know if I can."

He braces his forehead against mine, and the dock rocks us back and forth, as though we're dancing.

"I understand," he says, and those words are enough to make my knees buckle. I love the fact that he understands that I can't be pushed in this moment. I feel like I'm on a train speeding at two hundred miles an hour with no brakes. I need to think, and I can't do that around him.

"But that doesn't mean I have to like it," he finishes.

I smile and reach up on my tiptoes to kiss his

cheek in the moonlight, and then I step away, and he lets my hands slide from his. I turn and run down the dock, my footsteps echoing in the dark, and I know that no matter how far or fast I go, I can't erase the imprint of this night.

CHAPTER 14
shawn

What the hell?

I blame all that gunk she had on her face. Or the perfume—the perfume could have done it, too. It made the air around her smell like peaches. And something was different with her eyes; they were bluer than usual, her eyelashes longer. Fuck. Never in my life have I noticed a girl's eyelashes. As soon as I saw Rachel walk out of that party, I had to go. I made some lame excuse to Lexi, who was hanging on my arm. I think I said I had to take a shower or something, but it wasn't convincing because she looked pissed when I pulled away and left. It wasn't my greatest moment, but I didn't know what else to do. I had to go. So I followed Rachel all the way to the dock. She turned and looked at me and the moon sort of shone all over her hair and lit up her eyes. And then she was so soft against me, still smelling like peaches. She practically fell into my arms when I started kissing her. I never expected this. I'm in way over my head with Rachel, and we've kissed all of one time. I'm not sure what's happening with me or her or us, but I don't think I can stay away.

I've been busy all day with the arrival of our campers. Between getting them situated and starting the first day's activities, I haven't even had a glimpse of Rachel all day. There are ten of them in our cabin, a few of them here for music like myself. We've been doing icebreakers all morning, just trying to get to know each other. Now we're on the outdoor basketball courts, messing around in a free play period before lunch. I'm watching, chasing stray balls and keeping an eye on them when Jamie walks up.

"Dude."

He has that serious look on his face. I told him about what happened with Rachel last night and

I know he's been thinking about my predicament all day.

"Think about the position she's in," says Jamie. "If she admits she likes you, Lexi is going to kill her. And Lexi's her friend."

"I know, I know. I'm trying to chill. I'm just worked up about it for some reason. I wish Lexi would just get that I don't want her that way."

"She doesn't seem like the type of girl to get that hint."

"So, what's Rachel going to do?"

"Exactly my point, man."

This is exactly what I didn't want—a complicated situation. I kick at the dirt under my feet, staring out across the lake. Maybe this was all a big mistake. One of our campers comes up to me, a tall gangly kid with freckles, bumping me with his elbow.

"Are you going to play with us or what?" he asks, dribbling the ball at his feet. "You said we could have a two-on-two tournament before lunch."

I feel a surge of guilt. The last thing I want to do

is ignore my campers because I'm having some sort of stupid emotional hang-up.

"You're right," I say, and I snag the ball from him and carry it onto the court, already sorting out teams. "You're with me."

He grins so big I could fit the whole basketball in his mouth, and for the rest of our free time I'm too distracted to dwell on the events after the bonfire, at least until it's time for mess.

I stop Jamie as we approach the big double doors. "I can't go in there."

Jamie just rolls his eyes at me. "Are you scared to see Rachel?"

"No," I say, and I'm telling the truth. She shakes me up, but she's probably the least intimidating person I've ever known. "I don't want to see Lexi."

Now, Jamie grins at me.

"That actually makes sense," he says. "You'll know in about two seconds whether or not Rachel told her."

With that, he shoves me inside. I walk in, trying to act like I normally do, but searching desperately for any sign of a crazy redhead about to attack me. So far, so good. I start loading up my plate with potato salad and fried chicken. The cooks at camp are the absolute best. Luke used to be best friends with one of them, an old lady with pink glasses and a pink apron. She would sneak him extra cookies every single night. She's still here, actually. Whenever she pokes her head out of the bakery kitchen, I wave, and she always waves back. I look for her as I head for my table, but no luck.

I plop down next to Jamie, as always, and am about to take a giant bite of potato salad when Jamie hisses in my ear: "Incoming." I look up, and Lexi is prancing toward us. She has a Cheshire cat smile on her face, she's acting friendly, but I've got a feeling it's all smoke and mirrors. The question is, is she angry because I left her at the bonfire, or she is mad because her roommate and I made out and now she wants to kill me? I don't know whether to run or act casual. Privately, I wish I could do this without hurting anyone's feelings.

"Hey, there," says Lexi, her accent lengthening the vowels, and I tentatively think I'm off the hook.

"Hey, yourself," I say easily, turning toward her from the bench.

"We didn't get to finish our conversation last night," she says, pouting. She folds her arms and it pushes the edges of her lacy bra above her tank top.

"I know," I say, looking her in the eyes. "I'm sorry about that."

"It's fine," she shrugs, flipping her hair over her shoulder and giving me a smile. Down at her table at the other end of the room, I can feel Rachel's eyes shooting daggers at me, and it makes me feel better than I have since Rachel and I were on the dock together. I reach forward, tugging at the loops on Lexi's jeans shorts, and her eyes light up with excitement. Jamie is staring at me with his mouth wide open.

"Maybe we can choose a time to talk a little more," says Lexi, running her hands along my arms. She leans even closer to whisper in my ear, and I see

a few shocked looks from some of the other counselors. "I'm free anytime you are."

As she pulls back, Rachel appears out of nowhere.
I smile at her pleasantly. She gives new meaning to
the phrase, "If looks could kill." Her cheeks are spots
of red color.

"Shawn," she snaps. "Can I talk to you for a minute? Outside?" Before I can even open my mouth
she is stomping out of the mess hall, with Lexi and
Jamie both staring after her.

"What the hell?" mutters Lexi. She frowns,
looking at me, and I can see the wheels turning in
her mind.

"I think it's something about the volleyball tournament," I invent wildly, and Jamie follows up with
some story to Lexi, who seems somewhat convinced.
But her eyes are narrowed and I know she's suspi-
cious. I leave her in Jamie's capable hands and head
outside after Rachel.

I step outside the doors of the mess hall, and
Rachel is waiting to grab my arm and haul me away
down one of the trails leading through the forest. I

could easily pull myself free and walk away, but I let her drag me out of sight of the mess hall and the cabins. I've never seen her like this. Once we're out of sight, she turns on me.

"What in the *hell* was that?" she hisses at me. Her hands are on her hips, feet spread. She is a woman looking for a fight, and as she narrows her eyes at me my temper starts to flare, but fades again as I can't help but notice how magnificent she looks when she's angry.

"I was talking to a friend of mine," I say calmly, folding my arms and fighting a smile. "You haven't seemed to have an issue with that until today."

"You were talking to Lexi."

"So?"

"Don't act like you don't know why I'm angry," she says.

"You don't have a right yet to be angry at who I talk to."

"You were flirting with her."

"Well, well, well," I say, grinning at her. Her eyes narrow into slits. "You're jealous."

"I'm not jealous."

"It's okay to admit it, baby."

"I'm not your baby."

"But you want to be, don't you? Or else you wouldn't care who I flirt with."

She opens and closes her mouth like a fish, her hands balling into fists.

"Don't forget that it was you who ran from me the other night," I say, moving toward her. She backs away.

"I couldn't stay," she says. "I wanted to be honest with Lexi, but I can't."

"Good."

"Good! Good!" she throws her arms into the air. "You're insane. None of this is good."

"Oh, really? None of it?"

She almost smiles.

"No. It's complicated."

"Baby, you're making it complicated."

I'm inches from her now, towering over her, her head tilted sharply up so her eyes can meet mine. They are almost pure gray, no blue to be seen. She gets raincloud eyes when she's mad. Her mouth opens slightly, and her tongue comes out to lick her lips. I stand still in front of her, letting her make the call. Her eyes flick rapidly from my eyes to my mouth and back again, and I force myself to stay still.

"The hell with it." She spits the words out of her mouth and the next second she is in my arms, legs wrapped around my waist. She is kissing me as though she may never get the chance again, and I'm pulled in just like last night after the bonfire, a drowning man in a whirlpool. Her hair falls over our faces, like a dark curtain, and I smell peaches again and I dig my hands into her hips before I can help myself. Goddamn, she's wrapped around me so tight. I slide my hands down to grip her butt through her jean shorts, and I hear her whimper. We're both breathing hard now. I can feel her chest rising and falling against mine. She's pressed so close to me I can feel her heart hammering through both our shirts, and I want her closer to me. I pull her shirt out from where it's tucked into her shorts and finally my hands hit bare skin. Her mouth opens against mine and I slide my tongue against hers as my hands caress her bare lower back. She pulls away from me, bracing her hands on my chest. Her legs are wrapped around my waist and we're tangled in each other. I'm not even sure how she got all the way up here—she just leaped into my arms. We're both breathing like we just finished a marathon. Her hair is falling down, her eyes huge and dark as they stare into mine. I'm so hard that every little shift of her body on mine is torture.

"Um," she says.

"I know," I tell her, and I kiss her gently and set her on the ground. She stumbles a little as her feet touch down, but her glare tells me not to laugh so I bite the inside of my cheek and keep a straight face. Her gaze falls to my jeans and her lips part as she inhales. I know she can see how hard I am, and her cheeks flush but she meets my eyes.

"Are you going to run away again?" I ask her.

"No," she says. "But right now, I have to go."

I nod.

"We can meet sometime tomorrow," she says. "Okay?"

"Yeah, sure. Just send up a smoke signal or something."

She rolls her eyes at me and turns to go, but I pull her back to kiss her one more time, dropping kisses on her nose and cheeks as she tries to squirm away. She giggles and I finally turn her loose.

"Bye," she whispers, and she's off. I stand in the woods and I realize the sun is going down. I shove my hands into my pockets and wonder what I'm getting myself into.

CHAPTER 15
shawn

The next few days can be best described as cruel and unusual punishment. Rachel and I pass by each other over and over between camp activities, and each time we have to stroll past each other as though nothing at all is going on. It doesn't help that Lexi is watching her like a cat at a mouse hole. Every time the two are anywhere in my vicinity, Lexi is still all over me while Rachel stands awkwardly in the background. It's getting harder and harder to try and act casually around Lexi with Rachel standing right there. A few times, I've snagged Rachel while she had a moment to herself and it always ends with us kissing furiously and then jumping apart as soon as someone else comes along the path.

I'm headed back to the dock after coming off of a Music rotation, thinking about what's going to happen in the next few days. I think I'm going to go crazy; the few moments I've had with Rachel since that night on the lake haven't been even close to enough. The last time we ran into each other, we ended up in a heap in the bushes. Rachel's shirt was unbuttoned, her hair was a wild mess and my shirt was halfway off when we heard footsteps and sprung apart. I shake my head as I walk along the trail. If I don't see her soon, I think I might lose my mind.

The thought hasn't even had time to settle in my head before a familiar voice hisses at me from somewhere in the brush.

"Rachel?" I say quietly, and I see a flash of dark hair. Grinning, I look around to make sure no one is near and then head into the forest after her. I find her in the shade next to a huge oak tree with spreading branches.

"You heard me," she says in a whisper, smiling at

me. "I knew you'd be heading back from your Music rotation and I'm heading to the dock so I figured I'd try to snag you."

"Are you stalking me?" I ask, and Rachel starts to laugh and then throws a hand over her mouth.

"No, you arrogant jerk," she says in a whisper. "I just wanted to say hi."

"Is that all?" I ask in a low voice. I take a step toward her and watch her cheeks flush.

"Yes," she whispers. I grab the front of her shirt and pull her toward me. Her eyes light up. I skim my lips across her jawline and her eyelids flutter shut. The sunlight filters in through the oak leaves and dapples her skin. Her mouth finds mine and the frustration of the last few days erupts as our lips connect. Before I know what's happening, my hands are in her hair and her back is pressed against the tree. Her hands are gripping my wrists and then sliding their way down my shoulders and her mouth is a fire on mine. A few more moments pass and the rational part of my brain starts flashing an alarm. We both have places to be, as much I'd like to stay here with her the rest of the day.

"Rachel," I say. "We have to stop."

"No," she whispers, "Not yet."

I can't help but smile against her lips. I move to her neck, kissing my way from her jaw to her collarbone. She threads her arms around my neck and sighs into my ear and I don't know how I'm going to leave. We both pause, and I inhale the scent of peaches.

"Don't go," she whispers, and I kiss her cheek. I've never been into a girl like Rachel; a girl saying that to me normally would be enough to make me run in the other direction. But with Rachel, it just makes me want to pull her closer. Voices on the trail snap me back to reality and Rachel and I separate.

"I guess we really do have to go," she says.

"I don't want to either," I say. I wish I could promise her that I could meet her later, but this whole thing is so complicated that it's hard enough to snatch a few seconds as it is. She leans up and kisses me again and then pulls away, straightening her shirt.

"I better head back," I say, and she just nods, flashing me a small smile. I make my way back to the trail and start toward the dock like I didn't just spend five minutes in the brush getting myself worked up over a girl. I shove my hands in my pocket, and then reach up to brush off what feels like a branch from my shirt collar. This is getting out of hand.

CHAPTER 16
shawn

"**H**ey, cutie," I hear, and before I even turn around, a flash of annoyance spikes through me. I know who it is.

"Hi, Lexi," I say calmly, as she and Rachel walk up to where Jamie and I have our campers at the dock.

"I'm going to go and get everyone in the water," murmurs Rachel, and she herds their group of kids toward where a swim instructor has everyone in the water practicing freestyle. She bends over to dip her favorite tiny camper in the water, and I watch her butt until I realize Lexi is talking to me. In the few days since the campers have been here, I've seen

Rachel and that little girl together more than any other pair.

"What?" I say suddenly, realizing Lexi had said something I missed.

"I was just asking if you liked to ski," says Lexi, who appears not to notice I was just checking out another girl's ass. She's exhausted so many other questions that her ways of starting conversations with me are getting more and more random.

"I snowboard, actually," I say.

"Oh, I'm a skier. Do you wakeboard, too?"

"Yeah, I love to wakeboard," I say, relaxing into the conversation.

"Rachel and I are more lay out and tan kind of girls," says Lexi, putting her arm around Rachel's shoulder as she walks back toward us. "Right, Rach?"

"Huh?"

"I was just telling Shawn how we both prefer relaxing to water sports. Isn't that what you do when you're at the beach house in LA?"

"Oh, yeah, of course," says Rachel quickly, and I

think I see something flash over her face but I don't know what.

"I didn't know you had a beach house," I say.

"I tell her every day we need to make plans to come and visit," says Lexi. "Either the townhouse in New York, or the beach house. What do you think, Rach?"

"Oh, definitely," says Rachel brightly. "I'll check with my dad and see when he'll be in the country so he can take us out on the boat."

Lexi claps her hands together. "That sounds amazing."

"Yeah, it does," I say. Jesus. I forget that Rachel's family is so wealthy. I think of my mom and dad and our tiny blue house on the corner of the block. It's where I grew up, where Luke grew up, and it might be absolutely normal but it's perfect to me.

"I wish I could sit at my lake house every day of my life instead of going to college," sighs Lexi. "Do you have any plans for next year, Shawn?"

I resist the urge to roll my eyes. She's putting me

through an inquisition. What does she think she's doing? Sizing me up as husband material?

"I'm going to the University of Pennsylvania," I say.

Rachel perks her head up.

"Oh, wow," purrs Lexi. "What do you want to do?"

"I want to be a pediatric oncologist."

Rachel's eyes soften, and I know she knows why.

"Wow," breathes Lexi, staring at me like she's just seen the sun for the first time. "That's amazing. Is that like a cancer doctor?"

"Yes. For children."

"Wow. Any particular reason why?"

"Nope," I say quickly. "I like medicine, and I like kids, that's all."

I can see all the questions forming in Rachel's eyes, but I turn away.

"I've gotta keep helping Jamie," I say. "I'll talk to you guys later."

I walk away before Lexi can bombard me with any more questions. It's not that I mind so much, but

I hate answering them from her. Rachel should be asking me personal things like this, and she shouldn't be hearing it for the first time as I'm telling someone else. I yank my shirt over my head and dive deep into the cold green water of the lake, staying underwater until my lungs are about to burst. This whole situation is frustrating. I've got a girl I don't want who won't leave me alone, and the girl I do want only wants me in secret. I backstroke away from the dock. I didn't sign up for this. Rachel's dark hair waves on the dock, and I sigh as I tread water. I could back out now. I could tell her it's too weird for me. But even as the thought crosses my mind, I know I won't.

CHAPTER 17
shawn

"**H**ow's it going, man?"

Jamie comes up to me in the main cabin later that evening during a free period. I'm starting to get a sense of each individual kid's personality. I've already got names in my head for a few that are starting to stick out to me. Eagle Eyes is the fourteen-year-old who is constantly tripping over his own feet but somehow managed to pick out a doe and her fawn hiding in the brush from thirty yards away. Spotted Snout is the little freckled kid. He's already becoming known as the joker of the cabin. He is starting to remind me of Luke. When he used to come here with me in the summers, Luke would climb the flagpoles or a tree every time he got the chance. The counselors would come running, demanding he climb back down, but Luke just sat on a branch or wrapped his legs around the pole and watched for hawks. Hawks were his favorite. He loved to watch them swoop down to hunt or bank against the wind. For a second I swear I can see him there again, waving at me from the top of a tree while everyone else yelled frantically and I just laughed. He never fell.

"Fine," I say. "Why?"

"Just wondering how the whole situation was going. With Rachel."

I grunt.

"That good, huh? Alright then."

"I don't know what to do," I admit. "It's more complicated than I ever wanted it to be."

"So stop."

"No way."

I run a hand through my hair self-consciously, hoping it wasn't completely obvious how into Rachel I am.

Jamie grins at me.

"Then go after her. Stop playing around."

"She knows how I feel."

"Does she? She's just as frustrated as you are. She's probably wondering whether you even think she's worth it at this point."

Sometimes I hate hearing Jamie's advice because it seems like he's always right. And the idea of seeing Rachel is already pumping adrenaline through my body. I sit up and yank my shoes on.

"Can you take care of the campers for the rest of the night?"

"Yeah, dude. It's almost time for lights out, anyway. Go."

I'm already out the door, adrenaline coursing through my body. The sun has already set halfway down in the sky, and I can see stars beginning to flash. I notice the chill of the night, but I'm too energized to really feel it. All I can think about is getting to her.

Her cabin is already quiet: the little kids go to sleep earlier than the older ones. How am I going to do this? Lexi is probably in the room with her. I sneak around to the backside of the cabin where their room is and try to get a glimpse through the window. All I can see is Rachel's dark hair shining in the light. She has a book or something on her lap, but it's just sitting open while she stares at the wall. I don't see Lexi. Maybe she's in the main room of the cabin. I tap lightly on the glass, and Rachel spins around. Her cheeks turn bright pink, and she smiles so big it makes me laugh. I motion her toward me, and she nods, sliding the book under her pillow, and then she quietly opens the side door of the cabin while I go around to meet her.

"I wanted to see you," she starts, but her arms are already around my neck and my mouth cuts off her speech. My hands are already moving over her back, her hips, and she slides her hands into my hair, tilting my head so she can open my lips and tease me with her tongue. That night at the bonfire seems like such a distant memory—that shy girl standing on the dock has been replaced with someone who knows what she wants and is going after it full force.

I can't control the situation anymore. All I can do is try to keep up.

"Come with me," I whisper into her mouth, and I feel her head nod because her lips brush against mine.

"Let me make some excuse to Lexi," she whispers, and heads back inside. After a few moments, she comes back out, letting the door shut quietly behind her.

As soon as she's close enough to me, I pull her up against my body, and her hips land flush against my crotch. She looks down at me, then back into my eyes, and I know she can feel how hard I am. She shifts her hips against mine, like she's testing to see my reaction, and I groan and bury my face in her neck.

"Don't do that," I whisper, and she smiles against me before I turn and take her hand. I think she already knows where I'm leading her; she stays with me step for step. She links her fingers with mine.

"I heard what you said to Lexi today," she says softly. "About what you want to do."

"Yeah?"

"It's because of Luke, isn't it?"

"Yeah," I say. "Yeah, it is."

There is a twist, deep in my gut.

She leans up to kiss my cheek, and I lead her further along the trail, heading toward the lake. The moon is up now, but not as full as it was the night of the bonfire. I stop us on the shore at the same dock I followed her to that night.

"Do you trust me?" I ask her, and she looks at me and nods. I smile and pull her onto the dock, and she laughs as it rocks under our feet. She's so carefree and confident, different from the shy girl I first met, and I wonder briefly what's changed. We reach the end of the dock, and she turns to me.

"Thank you," she says.

"For what?"

"For everything," she says. "I've never really felt wanted in my life until you. Until this."

I don't know what to say. She looks up at me, the night sky reflected in her eyes and I kiss her until I feel her go limp in my arms. I meet her eyes and pull my shirt over my head. Her hands go tentatively to my stomach, tracing along my ribcage and down to my hips. I breathe in sharply when she tucks her fingers just inside the waistband of my boxers. I reach for the hem of her sweatshirt and she hesitates before lifting her hands above her head and letting me tug it off along with her tank top. Her bra is simple, white, her skin pale and smooth. She has a freckle at the swell of her breast. I reach for her shorts and pull her to me so I can kiss her collarbone. Her eyelashes brush my bare shoulder and I unbutton her jeans and let them slip down her legs. She steps out of them and buries her face in my shoulder. I can feel her trembling. I quickly unbutton and kick my jeans off and stand in my boxers in front of her. Her cheeks are bright red, but she scans my body with her eyes while I do the same to her. Her legs seem like they go on forever. I want to kiss her everywhere. I take her hand and turn to the water.

"Are you ready?" I ask her. She frowns.

"Huh?"

"We're going in."

"You're not going to pull me in the way you did last time. Shawn, it's freezing."

"You don't look cold to me."

"I'm not," she whispers, and I pull her to me, kissing her gently until she is breathless in my arms.

"Come swimming with me," I say, and she looks up at me again and just nods.

"On three?" I take her hand. She is already grinning.

"One, two . . . " I yank her hand, and she shrieks and grabs me and we both tumble into the water. The darkness closes over my head and I kick my way to the top where Rachel is already gasping for breath.

"You asshole," she says, but she is laughing and I pull her in by the waist and kiss her. Her skin is so warm beneath the chill of the water. I tread water and kiss my way down her neck while she gasps above me. Her bra strap has slipped down and I can't resist tugging the other one down and kissing her shoulder. She meets my eyes and reaches behind her and unhooks her bra and tosses it onto the dock. In the dark all I can see is the paleness of her skin and the pink tips of her breasts above the gentle waves. Her hair spreads into the water around us. I boost myself back up onto the dock and then reach for her, pulling her after me so she lands on top of me. She shivers in the cool air and I turn us both so she is lying on her back on the warm wood of the dock. I kiss her neck all the way down to the middle of her chest. Her hands dig into my hair and I can hear her breath coming faster as I lick the water droplets from the swells of her breasts. Her skin is unbelievably soft to the touch, like silk. I am so hard I feel like my whole body is going to explode. She is moving beneath me, pushing her hips toward me, and I run my tongue over her nipple and watch her eyes go unfocused. When I slide my hand into her panties, though, she stiffens.

"Are you okay?" I whisper, kissing her softly.

"Yes," she says, and I play with her hipbones, squeezing gently and then sliding my fingers lower. She presses her legs together and I can see the redness of her cheeks even in the dark.

"What's wrong?" I ask. I want her. I want her so

badly it's almost painful; stopping now isn't exactly easy, even though I know we've moved fast.

"I'm just, I don't—"

"What?"

"I've never done this before."

"Any of it?"

She shakes her head back and forth, still lying on the dock. Her feet are floating in the water. She sits up on an elbow and scoots farther back.

"I want to," she says. "I just . . . I don't know. I got scared."

To my dismay, tears well up in her raincloud eyes.

"Rachel, seriously, it's okay," I say, pulling her into my arms. She cries softly, warm tears mixing with the lake water that still covers both of us. She covers her face with her hands, and I wish I knew the right thing to say. I rub her naked back in small circles, and she reaches out and grabs her bra and clumsily puts the wet fabric back on her body. I wish she didn't feel the need to hide from me, but I can understand why she's overwhelmed. A week ago we barely knew each other, and this is a big jump from that. Especially for a virgin.

"Talk to me," I say. "What's wrong?"

She just shrugs against my body, wiping tears from her cheeks.

"It's just a lot to take in, I guess," she whispers.

I keep rubbing her back, wishing she would stop crying. I can't stand it.

"Maybe it would help if we got to know each other a little better," I say. She sniffles, but rubs her nose and nods again.

"Yeah, maybe," she says. "That sounds nice."

"Okay," I say slowly. "I'll start. I'm from Vermont. I've always lived there. My mom loves to play tennis and my dad is an elementary school teacher."

"Your mom doesn't work?"

"No, she used to but she stopped when Luke got sick."

Rachel nods against me, her wet hair brushing against my chest. I watch her long eyelashes blink. I'm desperate to make her stop crying, for her to know that she can trust me.

"How old were you?"

"When he got sick? I was fourteen. He was eight."

"You two were far apart in age."

"Yeah." I shift slightly. I'm not sure how I feel talking about this. It's not the easiest of subjects. "He was a surprise, as my mom put it."

"And then he passed away when you were sixteen?"

"Yes." I remember sitting with him in the hospital, the silence in the room as we all listened to Luke's ragged breathing. I hated being there, hated the sterile smells and the pale walls and the constant hum of the machines Luke needed.

We sit in quiet for a few moments. My chest aches just talking about Luke. It's one thing to have memory flashbacks when I'm alone, but to talk about him with someone else is completely different.

"You said you wrote about Luke," she says slowly.

"Yeah," I say. "I've never been a great creative writer—I've been playing music for so long that I never spent a lot of time on anything else."

"The opposite of me," says Rachel, smiling. "I

love music but never learned to play it myself. I would've liked to, but—"

She cuts off suddenly.

"What?" I ask, but her lips tighten and she just shrugs.

"I spent a lot of time on my school work," she says. "I was busy a lot."

"There wasn't time on the weekend for you to take lessons?"

"Not really," she says vaguely. I wish she would open up about herself a little more.

She shifts off of my lap and sits cross-legged on the dock, shivering. I hand her the sweatshirt I pulled off of her and she tugs it over her head.

"You're going to college in the fall?" I ask.

"Yes. The Vermont University for the Arts."

"What do you want to do?"

"I'm not sure," she says, running her hands through her long hair.

"You must have some idea," I say. I feel the need to know more about her since she already knows such an important and private fact about me.

"I just like to write," she says quietly. "I've written my whole life."

"Jamie noticed the ink on your arm on one of the first days here."

"Really?"

"Yeah. He mentioned it to me."

"Nobody ever notices me that way," she says, and her words pull at me.

"I did," I say, and she smiles at me. She looks perfect in the moonlight, her dark hair drying around her shoulders and her pale skin glowing, but she also looks delicate somehow, like she might blow away in the wind coming off the water. She shivers again, and I stand up and hand her shorts back as I pull my clothes on. I take her hand and she follows me willingly off the dock and back up the trail toward our cabins. The air is still and quiet, covered in cloud, so only slivers of moon and starlight can be seen. I stop in front of her cabin and she links her arms around my waist as I take her face in my hands and kiss her, tilting her face up toward mine. She makes a humming noise in her throat and every muscle in my body tightens. She opens her eyes and stares at me as I pull away with that look on her face again, as though she's seeing the sun for the first time.

"What is your cabin's schedule like tomorrow?" she asks. "I'm doing a Poetry unit with a group of campers after lunch and then I have a free period. If you get a free hour or so you should meet me and we can write together."

"I don't know," I say. My writing about Luke is intense and private. I don't want her criticizing it or trying to edit it; I write it for me.

"I would love to read some of your poems," she says quietly. "Just to read them."

I look into her eyes and I feel such a strong need to know more about her, too. She's the only one who knows about this part of me, and one of the only people here who knows about Luke. I feel so drawn to her because of that. Everything between us has moved so fast, but it's been so intense at the same time.

"Okay," I say. "I can probably find a free hour in

the afternoon. I'll see you tomorrow," I say, kissing her cheek.

"Goodnight," she whispers, and then she's running silently up the steps and into her and Lexi's room, and I'm left to walk back to my room alone. I wonder at the difference between the way I started the night and the way it ended. I definitely did not plan for it to unfold the way it did. I felt terrible when she got upset, but I do understand. I hope she knows she doesn't have to feel uncomfortable around me. I hope she's herself with me, because I feel like the deepest parts of me just tend to come out when I'm with her. I shove my hands into my pockets, wondering for the billionth time what I've gotten myself into.

CHAPTER 18
rachel

July 28ᵗʰ, 2014
I feel like an idiot. We were skinny dipping together, mostly naked, and I stopped him at the last minute. I feel like such a child. What kind of girl does that? I just got so scared. Everything was happening so fast and it was too overwhelming. I panicked. I barely know this guy. Last week I thought he was an asshole and now he's the only guy who's ever seen me that way. I'm not sure what's changed, but at the same time everything has. I've seen so much more of the person he is below the surface; he's sweet and passionate and maybe a little stubborn, sure, but I can match him for that. He's so much more than I thought he was. Every time

I hear him mention his little brother I just melt; it's the most heartbreaking story. I'm excited to see the words that come to the page when he writes about Luke; poetry is such a private endeavor, and I feel lucky that he's willing to open up that part of himself to me. It makes me feel privileged, as though we share a secret bond.

I still haven't told him the truth about myself.

With that, I close my journal and unfold my legs from where I'm curled on my bed. It's not a thought I want to dwell on right now, not while I'm so happy. It's early morning; the sun is barely rising over my window's edge. I've been up almost all night, sitting here writing about him, but I'm not tired. I feel like I've just had a bucket of espresso. There's adrenaline pumping in my veins and I can't stop smiling. I wish now, more than ever, that I hadn't stopped what was happening by the lake. I want more than anything to be the kind of girl that he wants. Next time, I won't hold back.

Lexi walks in from the bathroom, yawning hugely, and I'm flooded with guilt. It doesn't matter, I tell myself. It doesn't matter at all because she'll never have to know. Shawn and I can keep this a secret from everyone. I like the idea of keeping the whole thing private, though. I like being able to appreciate this little glow inside my chest that no one else knows about. I want to laugh out loud. Who am I? I've never been this girl before, the one who falls head over heels and winds up giving her whole heart to a guy. But I've never had someone who wanted to take it before. And now that I do, I never want to go back to the girl I was before this. I want to stay the way I feel now—so alive and special and new. I click the lock closed on my journal and slip it away into my backpack.

"What's got you looking so perky today?" asks Lexi as she gets dressed.

"I don't know," I lie glibly. "It just seems like a good day."

She just groans and goes into the main room to wake up the rest of the campers.

At mess, I fill my plate with bacon and eggs and sit down between Lexi and Sadie. Sadie is one of our six-year-old campers who has completely attached herself to me. From the first day they all arrived, she was sorted into our cabin and I knew we'd be friends. She is a dancer who, according to Lexi, has a lot of potential, even for being so young.

"What are you writing?" Sadie asks. She has blonde curls and bright blue eyes that watch my every move.

"Nothing, Monkey," I say. I decided on Monkey for her camp name since she's always hanging on me. "Just a little something."

"You write in there a lot."

"Oh, really?"

"Yes. Are you writing a book?"

"I guess you could put it a little like that."

"Can I read it someday?"

I laugh, noticing the way Lexi's eyes slant toward us.

"Maybe someday," I answer.

Sadie grins at me and goes back to eating her English muffin. I look across the room to where Shawn sits next to Jamie, his plate piled high with bacon and eggs, as usual.

After mess, Lexi pulls me right toward Shawn and

Jamie, and I know she's going to flirt with him, but somehow I just don't care.

"Hi, guys," she says. "What's on your agenda for today?"

As Jamie starts to answer her, I catch Shawn's eye and give him a small smile. He meets my eyes, smiling softly.

"What about you, Shawn?" Lexi continues. We're all walking toward the cabins, and she loops her arm through Shawn's and he doesn't fight it. A trickle of dread flows down my spine. We stop at the fork where the path splits off between male and female cabins, and I catch Jamie giving me a quick look of sympathy. My good mood has essentially evaporated.

"Okay, well we have to take the Otter Tails to arts and crafts," finishes Lexi. "But we can meet up with you guys later. Just let me know." And with that, she leans up and kisses Shawn on the cheek. My lungs feel as though they've just been crushed by a cement truck. I turn on numb legs as Lexi takes my arm and starts walking us back to the cabin. I wonder vaguely where the rest of our campers are, and then remember we sent them all ahead with Olivia leading.

"Someone had to make the first move," says Lexi, and she slants her eyes at me as though she's gauging my reaction to what she's just done. It's as though she's baiting me, waiting for me to admit what's going on, but I won't. She may suspect, but there's no way she knows for sure, and it's going to stay that way.

"Yeah, you're right," I say lightly. "I probably would've done the same thing."

"Oh yeah?" she says. "With all the guys back at home you have waiting for you?"

I look at Lexi and she has an expression on her face I've never seen. It's cold and calculating and it chills me to the bone. I am silent, unsure of what to say, and in the same second she snaps out of it, throwing her head back and laughing.

"I'm just teasing you," she says. "Don't look so serious."

But I have a feeling deep in my gut that she's not joking.

He doesn't even like you, I want to say. *He wants me. For once in my life, it's me. Not you.* But I can't bring myself to utter the words. However much it hurts for Lexi to keep on flirting with Shawn, she's still my friend. I still want to make it through this summer without ever having to explain this to her. I know I'm being dishonest, but at this point I don't even know where to begin. *Hey, I hated Shawn but then it turned out that I actually really like him and he's miraculously attracted to me too?* Even in my own head, it doesn't sound plausible. Everything that seemed so set in stone this morning looks different in the light somehow. I lock the thought away and follow Lexi up our cabin stairs.

Hours later, I've managed to banish thoughts of this morning as I sit with a group of campers and go through a basic poetry drill. We're seated at a wooden table in one of the smallest cabins. It's private and peaceful, sitting right on the edge of the little creek that flows into the lake. The windows are wide open with sunlight and fresh air pouring in. I hate working somewhere stuffy.

"Can I write about my kitty?" asks a tiny camper with dark curls and a little lisp on the *r*'s.

"Yes, of course you can," I say. "This exercise is about writing whatever comes to the forefront of your mind. You can never write about something wrong when it comes to poetry."

I sigh and press my hand to my piece of paper. My heart is so full, so many things waiting to spill out of it, but I don't know where to begin. I instruct the group to keep in mind that they should be considering what piece they are going to submit to the newsletter at the end of camp.

"You are all welcome to perform, as well," I say. "At the showcase. It's encouraged for anyone and everyone to take the chance to perform their work, or any other work of your choosing." The showcase is more about getting campers and counselors alike used to performing in front of an audience, so performing pieces other than your own is allowed.

At the look of panic in a few sets of eyes, I am quick to explain that the showcase is optional, and anyone can also submit their written work to the newsletter for it to be recognized. After another few drills, the campers are headed out the door to the next part of their schedule and I'm in the little cabin alone. I hear another set of footsteps, and a shadow floods the doorway.

"Hi," says Shawn quietly. Rays of sunlight bring out the flecks of green in his eyes.

"Hi," I say, and just like that, my anger and frustration toward him from this morning evaporate. All I care about is that he's here, standing in front of me, with eyes that express an apology.

"About this morning—" he starts, but I stop him.

"It doesn't matter," I say.

His brow furrows. "But, I just wanted to tell you—what happened, I didn't want—"

"I get it," I say. "Really, I do. I'm not mad."

"Oh. Well, okay then."

He shifts his feet, and I see the notebook in his hands. It's worn, like my journal.

"Do you want to get started?" I ask.

He looks up and meets my eyes, and I swear sparks ignite between us.

"Yeah," he says softly.

"Okay," I say, already breathless.

He pulls up a chair and sits down across from me at the little table. I pull my journal out of my backpack.

"Let's start with an exercise," I say. "Write about someone, or something, you love. I just did it with the campers before you got here."

"Okay," he says, brow already furrowing. He starts to write in the notebook, and I put my pen to my journal. After a few minutes, I ask him to give it to me.

"I'll just read it and see what feeling you put on the page," I explain. "You don't need to be nervous."

He shifts in his seat, and I know how hard it must be for him to share something so close to his heart. I wait, letting him decide, and he finally turns his notebook over to me. I read the words he wrote, skimming through them. The piece he's just written is brief and intense, but it's the poem on the opposite page that catches my attention. The piece of paper it's written on is wrinkled and the writing is smudged, like he wrote it a long time ago.

. . . I would spiral into your bloodstream
fill your spaces with my spaces
so you can carry me with you
wherever you go . . .

It's beautiful. I can't explain how beautiful. It's a short poem about loss and love, and it touches me to the core. I turn his notebook to that page and place it back down on the table.

"This is something you wrote awhile ago?" I ask, and Shawn runs a hand through his hair as his eyes skim the words.

"Yeah, that's an old one," he says. "You liked it?"

I nod.

"Yes. I loved it. What you just wrote was good, too, but that one was amazing. It's about Luke?"

"Yeah," he murmurs. "What it felt like to lose him."

"I'm sorry you had to feel that kind of pain," I say carefully, "but this really is amazing. Why don't you show others this? Why don't you perform it?"

"No way," he says immediately. "I don't want anyone else seeing this."

"Are you embarrassed?" I ask.

"No," he says. "No, I'm not. Maybe someday I'll feel ready to share it. But it's private."

"But someday, you'd consider it?"

He gazes at me, and finally shrugs.

"Sure. I guess."

He looks at me over the table and there is a connection between us, growing stronger and stronger. I am the only one who has seen this work, and even though I understand the need for privacy, I also want to share it with the world. The whole point of beauty like this is to share it, to let other people know how amazing it is. I know he doesn't seem like he's ready now, but sometimes it takes someone giving you a little push before you know for sure what you're capable of. God knows my mom would never even have been able to hold down a job as a waitress in a coffee shop if I hadn't pushed her to apply, then pushed her to get up and go everyday. I push myself constantly, to keep my grades up, to go to school every day, even when I feel like I can't stand another day there.

"Okay," is all I say. We run through a couple more drills, and the more I see of his work, the more impressed I am. It's simple, but powerful language, and even when it breaks my heart it touches me in a way that's indescribable.

"Can I see that one again?" I ask toward the end of the hour. "The one about Luke."

Shawn slides his notebook across the table, his eyes locked on mine.

"What are you doing with it?" he asks.

"I just want to keep it for a few days," I say. "It's so beautiful. Do you mind?"

His eyes lock onto mine, and he leans forward so his elbows are on the table. Somehow, just that simple motion is sexy when he does it.

"Okay," he says quietly.

"Thank you," I whisper as I lean across the table. I meet his lips with mine, just a gentle brush, but my heart hammers in my chest.

"Meet me later?" I ask, knowing the time we have now is ending. I want to see him tonight.

"I look forward to it," he says, giving me a lopsided grin. My heart begins to slam against the confines of my chest. This time, I won't freak out or be childish. I'll be confident. This is what I want, anyway. I know it is. No guy has ever made me feel like this before—like I'm wanted. We gather our things off the table and head out the door. He stops me as I'm about to head down the steps with a hand that snags my waist. He pulls me to him, kissing me hard and fast. I wind my arms around his neck and his hands slide into my hair until he breaks away, panting. I glance around, worried someone might have seen, but there is no one in sight.

"I'll see you tonight," he says in a low voice that sends a shiver through my body.

"Yes," I say, and he heads down the cabin steps

and down the path, disappearing from my sight. I sigh, watching him go.

A vibration in my back pocket jolts me back to the present, and I pull my phone out of my pocket.

"Hello?"

"Mercedes! Baby, how are you?"

"Hi, Mom," I say, irritated already since she's forgotten to call me Rachel. "Everything is good."

I don't have the heart to scold my mom for calling me instead of waiting for me to call her when I've been so busy I haven't had the time to call her first.

"Oh, how fun. Everything here is good, too. Pete has replaced you for the time being."

"Sounds great, Mom."

"You're awfully mellow today," she says suspiciously.

"Am I?"

"Yes. What's got you in such a good mood?"

"Nothing, Mom."

"It's a boy."

"It's not."

"Oh, Mercedes, it's obvious. What's going on? Has something happened? Tell me."

"Mom!" I'm too flustered to be mad at her for calling me by my real name. I can already feel my cheeks turning red, and I start down the steps away from the cabin. "First of all, it is absolutely none of your business."

"Oh, so nothing has really happened yet."

I rub my face with one hand, and seriously debate throwing my phone against a tree.

"Mom, I'm not talking about this with you."

"Is he a nice guy, at least? Does he deserve you?"

My heart softens a little bit.

"Yes, Mom," I say. "He's amazing."

"Do you love him?"

"I don't—I mean, I don't know if—"

"Alright, so you do."

I don't know what to say.

"Honey," my mom says softly. "I know you and I don't always see eye to eye when it comes to the male species."

The understatement of the year, I think.

"But I'm worried about you. Does this guy feel the same way about you?"

"Mom, I already told you I'm not discussing this with you."

The palms of my hands are starting to sweat. Of course I'm ready for this. Last night was just a fluke; I panicked. This night will be different. It'll be perfect.

"Just think about it, honey. Please. And besides, if he's another counselor, isn't there some rule against—"

"No one will know if anything happens anyway."

There is a pause.

She just doesn't understand. I know what I'm doing.

"Mom, I have to go. My free period is ending."

"Alright," she says, her voice quiet. "Just be careful, okay?"

"I will, Mom."

"Love you."

"Love you, too."

I click the phone off and head back to meet my

campers. I wish I could talk to her about everything that's happening, but my mom and I have never agreed on anything pertaining to men—she is right on that point. But I've never been the one with the guy before. It's new territory for everyone. I don't want her advice. I've taken care of her in addition to myself nearly all my life. All I've seen, year in and year out, are her dysfunctional relationships with guys.

I arrive back at the lake, where my campers and Lexi are waiting for me to help lead a short hike around the water's edge.

That evening, with Lexi asleep in the bed beside me, I hold my journal open on my lap. My pen lingers on the blank pages, drawing splashes of hearts and stars and suns, but no words come. I'm still not sure whether Lexi is onto Shawn and I or not, but since this morning she's been acting like nothing is wrong. I just don't know if I can trust her, even though I want to.

I am shaking, thinking about tonight. I'm

desperately tempted to just lie down in bed, pull the soft sheets over me, and call it a night, but then I call myself a coward. *You want this,* I tell myself, and it's true. My whole body is achy, needy, craving to be near him. It's my mind that's working overtime. *It's not that big of a deal,* I tell myself. *People do this everyday.* But I am still shaking when I get up and pull my shoes on. I yank my hair out of the ponytail and let it cascade down my back. My shadowed face in the mirror is pale, my eyes wide and clear. I am breathing hard, bringing color to my cheeks. I look like myself, but the reflection is still not one I recognize. This girl getting stars in her eyes over a boy has never been me before. But at the same time, I feel like my life is finally beginning, like an invisible switch has been flipped and now I'm finally, painfully, alive. I grab a thick blanket from the closet of our room and open the screen door. Lexi sleeps like a rock throughout the entire night: I don't have to worry about her waking up and realizing I'm gone. The air blows over my face, cooling my cheeks. It's cold out tonight, another reminder of autumn's impending arrival. Another thing I don't want to think about. The box in my mind that I use to store those kinds of thoughts feels full to bursting, but it doesn't matter. All I can think about now is seeing him. I jump down the steps and head toward his cabin.

CHAPTER 19

rachel

His lights are all off. It's late now; everyone is sleeping, leaving the camp with a strange, deserted feeling. I creep around to the back of his cabin the same way he did with me last night, and I flash back to his hands on my bare skin, the touch of the water, and his hands skimming my body. I tap gently on the window of his and Jaime's room, and the back door opens almost immediately. Shawn walks out. One hand is shoved into the front pocket of his jeans as he reaches around to close the door softly against the frame.

"Come here," he whispers to me, and I walk up the steps on legs that feel like clouds, clouds that are going to evaporate and let me fall any second. He wraps me in his arms and I bury my face in his shirt, just breathing him in. He kisses the top of my head, then my temple, then my nose, and I tilt my face up to him and then his mouth is on mine and everything I've been thinking about all day just fades away. Nothing is more important than this moment; nothing can get in the way of what is happening in my body and in my heart. He nudges my lips open, and his tongue caresses the inside of my cheek, my bottom lip. I reach up and wrap my arms around his neck, pulling myself as close to him as I can possibly get. My hips brush against his, and I can feel how hard he is already, and the knowledge gives me a little thrill deep within my body. He makes me feel powerful in a way I've never felt before in my life; it's exhilarating to see what I can do to him with my body, how much I can make him want me with just a touch. He pulls away, running his hands up and down my arms.

"You have a blanket," he says.

It's at our feet now, dropped when he first came out of the cabin.

"Yeah," I say, reaching down to pick it up. "I thought we could go lay it down somewhere."

I can see the flash of his smile in the darkness, and I can't help but grin in return.

"That sounds good to me," he murmurs. "Do you know where you're going?"

His voice calms me down and excites every part of my body at the same time. I just tug on his hand, and he follows me into the darkness. We walk along the main path for a while until we come to a fork, and I pull him to the left. An owl swoops overhead, a flash of white, and something else scurries in the brush to our right. The crickets are singing, and I can hear frogs down by the lake. Amid all the nighttime noise, my heart is beating so hard I'm surprised he can't hear it.

"Are you scared?" he asks me.

"A little," I say.

"Yeah, I probably would be, too, if I wasn't from

here. I guess you don't see a lot of owls or bears in New York or LA, huh?"

With a start, I realize he wasn't asking about tonight.

"Oh, the animals don't scare me," I say. "I love being able to come outside and be in so much open space. The city gets so crowded."

"I believe that," he says. "I've been to New York with my family a few times. It was a little chaotic for me. But I'm sure it would be different if I'd been with you. You could show me the best parts of New York."

I think of the beautiful parts of New York, the stores and the shops and the high-rise apartments nestled way up in golden lights. I can't show him that part of New York as anything but a stranger; it's completely different from where I live in the Bronx. But he'll never have to know that.

"What a touristy thing to say," I tease, and he tickles my ribs. We come to the clearing, and his feet stop behind me. It's just a little opening in the trees, lined with soft clover and sweet fern. The lake shimmers in the background, and through the openings in the leaves and branches, stars and clouds float in a black sky. I lay the blanket down, and it makes a soft dip in the clover. I hold out my hand and Shawn comes to sit down beside me. He pulls me onto his lap, kissing my cheek and I lay my head sideways on his chest. I am shy all of a sudden, and I pull my legs up to my chest.

"Relax," he whispers, shifting me around so I'm facing him. His lips ply mine as his hands run up my back, kneading my shoulders in a way that makes me want to moan. I fall against his chest, and he lies back on the blanket. My elbows are on either side of his head as I lay on his chest. Our eyes meet for a breathless moment before he reaches his head up to kiss me again. His hand holds the back of my head, pressing me possessively to him, and as I shift my body against his he groans into my mouth. He rolls us over so I'm the one on my back, and he is kissing me so fast it's turning me inside out. My head is spinning, and my body is all sensation, as though every single inch of my skin is attuned to what he's doing to me. He tugs my shirt up just an inch and kisses his way across my stomach, and I arch beneath him before reaching up to help pull his shirt over his head. Our hands are a blur as he pulls off my sweatpants while I'm unbuttoning his jeans at the same time, and then suddenly there isn't anything separating us anymore.

He brushes the back of his hand over my breasts, and everything goes gloriously blurry as I gasp. Meeting my eyes, he gently takes my hand and guides it to his body. Timidly, I explore his chest with my fingers, the smooth skin and ridges of hard muscle down to his stomach. He sucks in a breath as I trace his hardness and wrap my fingers around him. He scoots us down so we're both lying flat again, and then he trails a finger down my neck, around each of my breasts, and down the middle of my stomach, making my whole body quiver. He goes lower, circling my hips and finally dipping lower to the part of me that aches whenever I think about him. He strokes me gently, and I whimper and move against him, unused to the feeling spreading from the core of my body. I need him.

"Shawn," I whisper, "Shawn, please . . . "

He rises over me, nudging my legs apart with his, and digs into the pocket of his jeans and pulls out a silvery packet. He tears it open with his teeth and quickly puts it on as I watch. He looks so big now, and a first flash of fear floods through me. I am scared this is going to hurt. He leans back down, stroking the hair off my face, and his touch calms me. I'll be fine. I won't ruin this like I did the last time.

"Just try and relax," he whispers, and there is a pressure and then pain, so much pain. I grit my teeth and try to do as he says, but it's hard to relax your muscles when they're braced. He shifts, just a little, and more pain shoots through my body. I whimper despite my best efforts, and he looks down at me.

"Are you okay?"

"Yeah," I gasp, but I know he can hear the pain in my voice.

"Do you want to stop?"

I am not sure. I'm in a lot of pain, but I want to please him. I can do this.

"No," I say. "No, I'm okay."

He starts to move on top of me, and it still hurts, but the pain lessens in sharpness. I take a deep breath and he kisses my face.

"There you go, baby," he whispers. "Just relax."

I am so full, so intertwined with him. He increases in speed and I look up at the stars over his shoulder, my hands on his back. The pain fades into the background, and the scent of Shawn's skin comforts me. I kiss his shoulder lightly, and then he shudders, moans and then rests heavy on top of me. He kisses my neck, my cheek, and then lies still. I am a tangle of emotions, new and fresh and completely overwhelming. I'm glad he hasn't asked me how I feel because I wouldn't know how to answer. He tilts his forehead to mine and the rise and fall of his chest steadies mine. I lift a hand to his face, tracing his cheekbone with my fingers. He smiles at me. I smile back, surprised at how much just a look from him can calm me down. He lies back down on top of me, burying his face into my neck. I stare at the moon, the silent stars, and wish I were up there somewhere in the darkness where everything could become clear.

CHAPTER 20

shawn

"**S**hawn. Shaaaawn. Man, wake up."
I am lying flat on my bed in my boxers and a T-shirt, and I can hear Jamie, but I want to punch him rather than answer.

"Shawn. Seriously, man, I gotta talk to you."

I groan, and sit up slowly, rubbing my face with a hand.

"Man," I say. "It's not even time for mess yet."

The sun is coming up, but barely. It's got to be six a.m. The night comes back to me in a flood, and I remember tangling my hands in her hair, the way her back arched when I kissed her neck.

"Where did you go last night?" Jamie asks.

"Where do you think, man?"

"Did you . . . " he trails off suggestively.

"Yeah," I say quietly. "Yeah, we did."

"Holy shit."

"I know."

"But Lexi . . . "

"I know."

"What are you going to do?"

"I don't know. Rachel wants it to stay a secret, so keep your mouth shut."

"Of course. You two would be in so much trouble if anyone found out."

"Exactly."

Jamie leans back onto his pillow. "Wow. I didn't know you guys were that, well, serious."

"I don't really know how serious we are," I say honestly. "It's complicated. We hooked up, but everything is a secret, and we live in totally separate places."

"Camp ends in, like, a week," says Jamie quietly.

"I know, man, I know. And then we're going our separate ways. I guess."

As I say the words, there is a stinging in my chest. I know it's what makes the most sense, but I think of the look on her face last night, the way her eyes lit up when I walked into the cabin yesterday, and I know this is going to be hard. I'm attached to her, really attached. She's so different than any other girl I've ever known.

"That sounds complicated," says Jamie.

"She's a virgin."

"She is?"

"Well . . . she was."

"Fuck." Jamie's eyes are huge. "That's even worse. That's big time."

"You were right when you said complicated."

I hold my head in my hands. Lack of sleep is starting to take its toll. I need coffee, and I need to figure this out. I don't want to hurt Rachel at all. I would do anything not to hurt her.

We wake everyone up and head to mess, and I eat in a haze, gulping coffee. I don't see Rachel come in with her campers, but I'm a little distracted by everything going on in my head. Just thinking about it gets me worked up. She was really quiet afterward, though. I walked her back to her cabin and she kissed me and went inside. Now that I think about it, I'm not sure she said anything at all once we were finished. I hope she's okay. I wish I could just go and ask her about it, but we both have full days.

"Let's head out, Bear Claws!" yells Jamie, and I stand up to help lead everyone out to our first activity of the day. As we walk out the door, I see a flash of red hair, and my hands curl into fists. I cannot deal with Lexi right now.

"Hi, Shawn," she says, tossing her hair over her shoulder. For the first time, I notice she's already got her makeup on for the day. It's, what, eight in the morning? I don't pretend to understand everything girls do, but that seems a little extreme to me at a summer camp.

"Hi, Lexi," I say, continuing to follow Jamie and my campers.

"I need to talk to you," she says. I stop walking, surprised. She looks serious.

"Right now?" I ask.

"Meet me at lunch. In front of your cabin."

She walks away, glancing at me over her shoulder.

I frown, confused. What could Lexi possibly need to talk to me about?

Rachel arrives when Jamie and I are splitting up into groups for swimming and archery, and my heart lifts. I was starting to worry that last night had been too much for her. It was intense, and I definitely don't want her to withdraw from me because it was too much to deal with. Jamie nods at me and herds the group toward the activities, giving us a brief window of privacy.

"Hi," says Rachel, giving me a smile. "I just wanted to see you really quick before I head to a Poetry rotation." She is wearing a gray Maple Leaf tank top and jean shorts and her hair is in a ponytail. I can't help but grin. Everything about her is so much more understated than Lexi, and I like it much more than Lexi's overly made-up look and dramatic attitude.

I fold her into my arms. She links her arms around my waist.

"How are you feeling?" I ask. "From last night?"

"Oh," she says, and her cheeks flush pink. "I'm okay. I'm a little, you know, sore."

"Not too bad?"

"It's not too bad, no." She burrows her head into my chest.

We stand in silence for a moment, and I just enjoy the feeling of her in my arms again. I wish things were different, that she and Lexi weren't friends, that everything was just a little more simple.

"You know, I think I decided what I'm going to read for the showcase," she says quietly.

"Oh, really? What?"

I am honestly interested. I loved reading her poetry the other day.

"It's a surprise," she says, crinkling her nose.

"You won't tell me?"

"Nope," she says. "But I think you'll like it."

"I'm sure I will," I murmur, leaning down to kiss her neck. "I gotta go."

"Me too," she says. She kisses me goodbye and leaves, and I realize I forgot to tell her what Lexi said to me this morning.

After a few hours of swimming and archery with Jamie and my campers, they head to the mess hall for lunch and I head back to the cabin to hear whatever Lexi has to say. I hope it's brief, since I still need to eat. I honestly have no idea what she's going to say, but my bet is that she tells me off. I'm not looking forward to listening to her, but if she can get it off her chest and leave me alone from now on, it would be worth it. As I walk toward the front of our cabin, I see Lexi walking up the steps. I join her on the porch, standing in the shade of the overhang. She folds her arms as I walk toward her.

"What's going on?" I ask. "What do you need to tell me?"

She is quiet for a moment, her hands shoved in her back pockets. She looks me in the eye, and she isn't flirty or sweet, but cold. I barely recognize her.

"It's about Rachel," she says, and I consider acting innocent. Before I say anything, Lexi beats me to it.

"Don't even think about trying to deny it," she hisses. "I know about you two. I've known for a while, ever since she pulled you out of the mess hall."

I let her talk, unwilling to deny the truth, but I feel sick at the thought that she knows.

"Anyway," she continues, "that's beside the point. There are things you don't know about her."

"You think you know more about her than I do?"

"I don't think either of us knows her very well."

"What are you talking about?"

"I read her journal."

"No way," I say. "I've seen Rachel's journal. It has a lock, and she carries that key around with her all the time."

"It opens pretty easily with a bobby pin, too."

I am floored that Lexi would go so far to prove a point.

"You had no right to do that," I say. "That's seriously fucked up of you."

Lexi tosses her hair, her eyes flashing.

"Whatever. What's important is that I know the truth."

"And what would the truth be, Lexi?" I can feel myself getting worked up, and I try to remain in control. What right does Lexi have to try and get between Rachel and I?

"She's lied about her whole life to you," she says. "To all of us. She's dirt poor. She has no friends. I think I even read somewhere in there that Rachel isn't her real name. She doesn't even know who her father is."

"What?" My stomach dips and rolls, like I'm stuck on some kind of sick roller coaster I can't escape from.

"Yeah. She lives with her mom, who runs around with a different guy every day of the week. They live in a shitty apartment in the Bronx."

Everything is blurred, like Lexi's words are running through my mind in slow motion. But it's like they're not really sinking in. I don't want to believe what I'm hearing. I've told Rachel some of the most personal things about myself, and to think she's been lying this entire time about who she is kills me. But at the same time, if her life really was miserable, I can't blame her for not wanting to talk about it, or for lying. I know what it's like to wish a part of my life hadn't existed. I'm angry, but a part of me also understands. I need time to process this. Can I even trust Lexi? I run a hand through my hair and walk across the porch, trying to get my mind around what she's just told me.

"I just thought you should know," says Lexi, and I turn on her.

"Don't act like you did this for me," I say. "You did this for yourself, so you could break us up like you've wanted to since the second you knew."

Lexi gapes at me, a frown creasing her features.

"That's a lie," she says, but an ugly red flush is creeping up her neck and I know I'm right.

"You're pathetic," I say, turning away from her.

"Well, you're insane," she splutters. "She's been lying to you!"

"Stay the fuck out of her business," I say, taking a step toward her. "And stay away from me."

I turn and bolt down the steps, leaving Lexi standing at the top, still standing with her mouth wide open.

CHAPTER 21
shawn

Rachel finds me that evening as I'm heading back to my cabin. She's waiting just outside the door to my room, out of sight of the trail. Her dark hair is spread over her shoulder, her long legs curving into her jeans shorts. We've all been sunburned and scraped and God knows I've been bitten by more bugs on this trip than I can count, but Rachel somehow looks perfect.

"Hey," she says quietly, linking her arms around my waist the way she did this morning. "I was hoping to catch you."

I wrap my arms around her in turn, kissing the top of her head. All day, I've wrestled with what

Lexi's told me, but now that I'm with Rachel, my mind blurs. A part of me wonders what kind of life this girl lives behind the façade she shows us, and another part of me is just happy to have her close. I debate whether or not to bring up the conversation I had earlier, but when she reaches up and presses her lips to mine I lose my rational train of thought. She brushes her lips over me, teasing touches that make me pull her tighter. Her hands trace their way up my back, slipping underneath my shirt, and I groan when she hits my bare skin. She pulls away and takes my hand and I have no choice but to follow her. She leads me to where I now think of as "our place," that clearing off the path filled with clover. I can hear her breath mingling with the rustles and chirps of the night.

Rachel stops, turning to face me, and takes the hem of my shirt in her hands. We're both breathing hard now, and my blood feels like it's running faster every time her fingers brush my skin. She skims her lips across my chest and I grip her hair in my hands.

"Rachel . . . " I say, just her name, and her mouth

is on mine and I swear the heat between us is burning right through me. For a moment I remember Lexi's words and wonder what her real name is, and why she would hide that from me, but the thought disappears as soon as it arrives. I don't really know how to describe it, but being with Rachel eclipses everything else. I grip her hips and tug her shirt off as she works at my jeans. A few breathless moments and our clothes are in a pile and all I can see is Rachel's skin, like moonlight shining in the dark. Her eyes are huge and dark, but fearless. She steps toward me in that shy, serious way she has and I lose myself in her.

Afterward, I'm holding Rachel as she lies on my chest on our blanket in the woods. My heart is still pounding, and my body is tangled in hers. Our clothes are still scattered in the leaves, and her arms are wrapped around me. I'm stroking her shoulder slowly, watching her chest rise and fall. I'm wrestling with what Lexi told me, and I still don't know what to do about it. I could just ask her to tell me the truth, but I'm still smarting that she didn't trust me enough to tell me the truth about herself on her own. I've told her about Luke, about writing about him, and she's lied about her past the entire time I've known her. But as I'm holding her I face the same dilemma I did earlier: I don't know what this girl has been through or why she's been lying. All I know is the happy girl lying in my arms is someone I care about, and someone I want to keep happy. I have no idea how her and I are going to end up or what's going to happen, but I won't judge her.

She sighs, reaching up to kiss my neck, and all I can do is hold her tighter.

CHAPTER 22
rachel

'm so excited to perform at the showcase. And I'm never excited to perform—it scares me to death, actually. But tonight will be different. I want to hug myself thinking about what I have planned, but I resist the urge to talk about it or even write about it. I just hold it inside myself, a secret flame.

"Morning," I say to Lexi as we get ready to take our cabin to mess, but she just nods at me. She's been so cold the last couple of days, and she hasn't been flirting with Shawn. I have no idea why, but I'm not sorry to see the flirting stop. It was driving me insane. As we walk to mess, I think about Shawn. Tomorrow, camp ends: I have to go back to New York, and Shawn will go back home, too. There is a twinge in my heart; I don't want this to end. I'm hoping that tonight will make him see that we belong together, that there is some way we can work things out even with our different lives. I've never connected with someone the way I have with him, ever. My body is more and more in tune with his every day, and every day I feel more comfortable around him. And more than that, tonight, I need to come clean about my past, and hope he understands. I can't let camp end without him knowing the truth. It makes me cringe, the thought of him knowing the truth about my past, but I owe him that much.

I spend most of the day with the campers who will be reciting their poems tonight. Some of the younger ones are so nervous that it takes me forever to reassure them. Everyone is starting to pack themselves into the theater, a huge, open cabin with enormous vaulted ceilings and a stage for performances. Rows of chairs have been set up in front of the stage, and huge drapes cover the normally open windows. I'm standing in front of the stage, directing a few of my poets, when I feel a pair of hands sneak around my waist.

"Hey," Shawn whispers, kissing my hair. "Are you nervous?"

"Yes," I answer, smiling as I link my fingers through his. I look around surreptitiously, but I don't see any other counselors around besides us.

"What about you?" I ask. "You're playing a sax solo, aren't you?"

"Yeah," he says, "but it's nothing I haven't done before. No big deal."

I admire his ability to perform without a qualm of fear. I admire a lot of things about him. He tilts my chin up.

"I don't want this summer to end," I whisper, and a flash of pain crosses his face.

"Neither do I, baby," he whispers, and wraps me in his arms. I close my eyes, letting myself pretend that I never have to leave.

All too soon, it's dark outside, and I'm standing backstage in a black dress. My hair is straight, hanging down my back, and I'm clutching a crumpled poem in my hand, but I don't need it. I've looked at it a million times in the past week; I know every word by heart. For the last time, I wonder if I'm doing the right thing, but I can't help but do what I'm about to. I hear my name and step onstage, letting my eyes adjust to the spotlight. The crowd is just a faceless black smudge in the background. All I can process is my thundering heart and the blinding lights. I know that Shawn is out there somewhere, and all I can think is I hope he understands why I'm doing this.

"This is a poem that a good friend of mine wrote," I begin. "And I wanted to share it with all of you tonight. I hope you love it as much as I do."

My voice is shaky, but steadies as I begin to read:

" . . . *I would spiral into your bloodstream*
fill your spaces with my spaces
so you can carry me with you
wherever you go . . .

"Thank you," I finish, and I leave the stage to the sound of applause.

It's a short poem, so I'm off the stage again within a minute. I can barely breathe. I hate performing in front of other people in any sense, but I'm still waiting to hear Shawn's response. I think he'll be a little surprised, maybe even defensive at first, but he has to be pleased that I chose to read his poem. People are already coming up to me, congratulating me. I never said who actually wrote the poem—so at least no one but Shawn and I really know who wrote it. And as soon as I think his name, there he is. He walks up the steps to the backstage area and heads straight for me. I smile, walking toward him, and he stops me with a hand on my shoulder.

"Can I talk to you?" he says, and I hear the edge in his voice.

"Sure," I say, and he immediately turns and heads to the door leading out of the theater. I can feel the tendrils of ice sneaking into my fingers, but I'm sure it's fine. He's probably just surprised.

The air outside is cold and crisp, showing our

breath in wisps of white. Shawn turns to me and my heart falls as I see his expression.

"Shawn—" I start, and he holds up a hand.

"What the hell were you thinking?" he asks in a low voice. "That was my poem."

"Yes, I know it was," I say, "I never said I wrote it—"

"No, you didn't write it," he continues. "I did. I don't care about getting the fucking credit, Rachel. I care that I shared something personal with you and you couldn't respect that enough to keep it private."

"That's not true!" I protest wildly. "Shawn, everyone loved it. People were already coming up to me and telling me how amazing it was."

"I don't care," he says, and I knew, now, how wrong I had been, but all I wanted was for him to know how much his writing touched me.

"It was the most beautiful thing I've ever read in my life," I say honestly. "And I knew how personal it was to you—that's why I never said it was your poem."

"That's not enough," he says quietly. He's standing

in front of me in a dress shirt and black pants, hands in his pockets, not touching me. The glow from a crescent moon plays over his features, letting me memorize them in the fleeting light.

"Shawn, please," I whisper. "I never did this to hurt you."

"I wasn't ready for anyone but you to hear any of that," says Shawn. "That was personal and private."

Tears are falling now, blurring my vision, and I wish I could take it all back, but it's too late. I thought he might be surprised, maybe even angry at first, but then he'd see that I only did it because seeing his heart on the page was so blindingly perfect that all I could think of reciting on that stage were his words, so that maybe he would see how perfect they were too. Even as I try and rationalize it to myself, it starts to sound stupid. I did not think this through.

"You know what hurts even more?" he says hollowly. "Is that I shared that part of me with you, and you couldn't do the same for me."

What is he talking about?

"Please," I say again. "Forgive me. I just wanted to share it. It was too beautiful to keep hidden."

"That wasn't your choice to make," he says. I see the twisted pain on his face and I wish I could erase it as he walks away from me, leaving me alone in the dark.

CHAPTER 23
rachel

I walk back to my cabin because I don't know where else to go. When I get to our room, Lexi is already there, packing. She takes one look at my tear-stained face and starts laughing. I stop in my tracks, confused.

"Did something happen with Shawn?" she asks, and I freeze. His words play back to me and my heart sinks even further. Lexi has something to do with this.

"You know about Shawn?" I ask, and she laughs again in a high-pitched cackle that makes the hair on my neck stand on end.

"Well, well," she says, tossing clothes into her

suitcase. "Here I am thinking I failed this whole time, and here you are."

"What?" I whisper.

"I told Shawn the truth about you," she says, eyeing me with a cold stare. "He didn't care. He said he cared about you anyway." She rolls her eyes, throwing a pair of sandals into her suitcase. "I see now, though, that you've managed to do my work for me."

"How did you know?" I say, horrified. "What do you mean?"

I am falling somewhere, sinking fast into quicksand, with nothing to save me.

"Your journal," she says. "It's always tucked under your pillow when you don't have it." She strolls over to my bed and digs it out from under my pillow. I'm frozen in place, trying to process her words.

"There's a lock," I whisper, confusion and dread flashing through me.

"Like I told Shawn," Lexi says, "a bobby pin works just as well as your stupid key."

Every part of me goes cold, and then hot again.

I don't want to believe it, but I think of Shawn walking away from me and I see the snarl on Lexi's face and I know it is true. I think of all the deeply personal details it holds and a shiver of anger and disgust runs down my spine.

"You had no right to read that," I say.

"Please," says Lexi. "You've been fucking him this whole time, and lying to me about it. Lying to everyone about it, actually. As soon as I knew, I knew there'd be other things you were lying about. Not only that, you've been lying to everyone. You don't have a house in the Hamptons or in LA. You live in the worst part of New York in a dirty apartment with your mom, who's a whore."

I lunge forward and rip the journal from her hands. We stare at each other for a long moment as the horror of what she's said sinks in.

With that, she spins and leaves the room, slamming the screen door behind her. I sink to my knees as my legs fold beneath me. I am still clutching my journal in my hands. My mind is a blur of shock and pain, and my entire body is starting to tremble. I am filled with embarrassment and deep, deep shame. Suddenly, every decision I've made this summer seems wrong. I don't know what to do. I am so completely lost. I curl into a ball on the floor, staring up at the ceiling as the tears blur my eyes.

CHAPTER 24
shawn

'm sitting in my room with Jamie, still sifting through the night's events. I was thrilled to watch Rachel walk onstage, that dress flowing behind her. Then she started reading, and her voice started out so quiet, but grew stronger and stronger, and I knew she was reading my poem. About Luke. Dammit, that's what hurts the most—that poem was about Luke, something only she knew, when everything I knew about her was a lie.

"What she did was messed up," Jamie says quietly. "But, man, I think what she did came from a good place."

"How the fuck can you say that?" I ask, looking at Jamie. "How did this come from a good place?"

Jamie shrugs.

"It sounds like she's been taking care of herself her whole life," says Jamie. "Maybe this was her way of taking care of you, trying to help you heal."

I shake my head, but his words ring in my ears. Maybe Jamie is right, maybe this is her way of trying to help me take the next step toward moving on from Luke. But what she took from me and shared with all of camp was so personal that even if her motives were good, the execution was so bad that I don't know if I can forgive her.

"I don't know if I can get over this," I say honestly. I run a hand through my hair and lean my elbows on my knees.

Jamie just lays a hand on my shoulder for a long minute and then lies down in his own bed, giving me my privacy. I wrestle with tonight's events in my head over and over again. I'm so angry with Rachel, but I picture her eyes, gray in the moonlight and shiny with tears, and my gut wrenches. She definitely did not go about this in the right way, but I can't help but hope that she wasn't lying when she said she never meant to hurt me. I don't know when it happened, but it's suddenly more important for her to be okay than for me to be okay. I stand up and throw the door open to my cabin, heading out into the cold.

CHAPTER 25
rachel

'm still sitting in the middle of my floor when I hear footsteps. I think it's Lexi, coming back from wherever she ran off to, and I lift my head as the door opens. Shawn walks in with slow steps. He's still wearing his black pants and button-down shirt, and he looks so good it hurts. His eyes are serious. As soon as I see him, my eyes well with tears all over again. I am so humiliated I can barely make eye contact with him—he has known everything about me and still treated me as though he loves me. He didn't even get angry with me until tonight, when he felt as though I'd betrayed him. The realization humbles me, and I know how badly I've messed up.

"What are you doing here?" I whisper, brushing my tears. I shakily stand up and sit on the edge of my bed. Shawn stays by the doorway, watching me.

"I'm so angry," he says, and I drop my eyes. "I let you see a part of me that no one else has, and you betrayed that trust."

"I know," I say miserably. "I know, and I'm so sorry. I didn't mean for you to see it that way. I was just trying to help, to help you see how when you write about Luke it helps you heal. And it's so beautiful, Shawn, it made my heart ache. But I'm sorry."

"I know you are," he murmurs. "I believe that."

There is a quiet pause.

"Lexi told me what she told you," I whisper, my breath catching in sobs in my throat, and the tears fall in rivers down my cheeks. "I was going to tell you tonight, but she beat me to it."

Shawn walks toward me with slow steps, coming to sit beside me.

"You didn't need to lie to me," he says, and my chest feels like it's going to burst open. "But I never judged you for that. I cared about the person you were underneath."

I nod, broken, reaching for his hand, desperate just to touch him. He doesn't pull away.

"I'm so sorry," I whisper, and Shawn brushes my hair from my face. I turn to him, blinking through my tears.

"I'm not saying it's okay," he says, "but I think I understand where your reasons came from a little better now. Why didn't you just ask me if you could read it?"

I shrug.

"Honestly, I've been doing things myself for so long that I didn't even consider it," I say. "I'm used to making things happen on my own."

Shawn tilts his forehead to mine and laces our fingers together. My heart is swelling. I know I've messed up in so many ways, but I've never believed someone could care about me the way Shawn does.

"I can't believe you came back," I say, and Shawn chuckles.

"I couldn't leave without telling you it was going

to be okay," he says. "I know we've only known each other for a few weeks, but you've changed my life. I needed you to know that."

"Me too," I say. "You have no idea how much it means to hear you say that."

His arms wrap around me, holding me tight, and I lay my head on his shoulder. I know that I'm not perfect, and neither is he, and we can never hope to be, but in that moment, I know that together we are something brighter, more infinite. As our lips meet and bodies touch, I have the strangest feeling that no matter what happens with us after this night ends, we will never lose what we hold between us. Even the briefness of our time is threaded with little pieces of infinity, bright and glimmering, that will always lead us back to each other.